A KILLING IN THE WOODS

A BRIAR REEF MURDER MYSTERY

JORDAN SILVER

CHAPTER 1

"Umm, how are you always so good at this?" Sonya Davis ran her hands up and down her lover's back as she moved her hips up to meet his. His cock slid deep within her, and deeper still, making her juices run down and wet the place beneath her, soaking her ass in the bargain.

She's never been this wet with anyone else, never enjoyed the pleasures that this one man can give her. Her heart cried out as her loins trembled and she begged him in hushed whispers to go deeper. He took her lips roughly, bruising them with his brute force. A force she craved like water needed to quench a thirst.

His lips fell away from hers and made their way down to her neck where he teased her with his teeth, knowing that he didn't dare mark her. But knowing it, the thought of doing it still, filled him with a kind of excitement that he hadn't enjoyed in too long to remember.

She tugged his head back to hers as she felt her pussy

clench in readiness and their lips came together in fiery passion as they each tried to consume the other in the heat of lust. "Fuck me lover, fuck your woman, harder, harder, fuck me harder." She moaned the words against his mouth as he fucked into her harder at her command.

The two bodies moved wildly together on the blanket as they neared climax, neither of them giving much thought to the strands of hay that made their way through the threadbare material that had seen much better days.

Their naked bodies glistened in the bright sunlight that peeped through the lone dusty window as he pounded into her fecund flesh. This wasn't the first time they'd been here like this, and if they had their way it wouldn't be the last.

He pulled their lips apart when they both needed to catch their breath and she screamed out when his cock found her sweet spot. He covered her mouth with his big work roughened hand. "Shh, you'll get us caught."

"Then stop hitting my spot like that." She laughed teasingly and wrapped her toned legs around his ass, pulling his pounding cock harder into her.

"Now shut up and fuck me you beast." He replaced his hand with his lips once more, driving his tongue into her mouth in tempo with his thick long cock that reached her depths with each thrust.

She'd never been fucked so hard or so well before in her life and her heart was full to overflowing. A sexual being all her life, she reveled in the fact that she'd finally found someone who could fulfill her needs over and over again.

Always before she'd have to go away in her head, pretend to be with someone else, doing any manner of things just to get off.

But not with him. In the year and a half since they'd

been fucking he never once let her down and she never wanted it to end, never wanted to be without him.

"When are you going to leave her?"

"When are you going to leave him?" The answer was never. It was just part of the game they played with each other, talking about their individual spouses while they fucked each other blind.

It added some extra spice to their passion, made it even more exciting. Added to the risk they were taking, it made for some very explosive orgasms, for him and for her. The element of the forbidden gave them both a thrill.

"Cum inside me."

"Are you sure?" He felt his balls tighten up in preparation. She's never let him cum in her without a condom before; every time he fucked her raw she made him pull out and cum on her ass or her flat tummy.

"Yes, I'm sure, cum in me. Let's take the risk." The thrill, the excitement, it was too much for her and she came screaming into his mouth as he emptied his seed inside her for the first time that day.

He stayed on top of her until he'd given her the last drop, then rolled away and reached for his discarded flannel shirt to retrieve his pack of cigarettes. "You want one?"

"You know I do."

She only smokes at times like this, in between bouts of shared passion with him, only him. In her real life she wouldn't dare; not the upstanding wife of one of the town's leading citizens.

Mother, friend, confidant; member of the PTA, head of the local charity and all around good girl, here is the only place she felt free to let her hair down. Here, or any place they could find to be alone together.

"You know I'm going to fuck you again, you don't need to be anywhere do you?"

"Nope, I have the whole day set aside just for you." He lit one cigarette and passed it to her before lighting another for himself.

They laid in silence, blowing smoke in the air as they relaxed in the afterglow of what they'd shared. He rolled to his side facing her, his finger making a trail down her middle until it met her Mons.

"You have the prettiest pussy I've ever seen." She opened her legs when his hand moved lower giving him free access to her. He dipped his finger inside as she lifted her lips to his.

The kiss was deep, soul stirring as she rolled over on top of him, making sure to keep the burning cigarette away from his eyes while reaching between them with her free hand to find his already rising cock.

With a few strokes of her hand he was stiff again as she rubbed the fat head back and forth along her slit. Each time the bulbous head of his cock touched her clit she felt a shiver run down her spine.

He moved her hand away, taking over, no longer willing to wait and forced his cock inside her. She released air from her lungs as he pulled her down on his cock until her ass hit his thighs and his balls were squeezed up tight against her ass cheeks.

They both put the cigarettes out hurriedly to avoid starting a blaze in the dry hay and she planted her hands on his chest as she rocked her hips back and forth, taking him in deep. "I want you to fuck me from behind, I love the way you do that."

She panted out her need as she fucked herself hard up and down on his cock. He tweaked her clit between his

4

fingers to bring her off before lifting her off of him and putting her on her hands and knees.

She screamed out in pleasure pain when he drove his cock into her without warning and this time when he covered her mouth with his hand he pulled her head back until her neck couldn't go any further.

His hips pounded faster, harder, slapping against hers as his cock reached places inside her only this position could achieve. "Yes-yes-yes I'm cumming, I'm cumming; you make me cum so good." Her words were muffled against his palm as her eyes rolled back in her head.

He covered her lips with his as he pounded out his lust and once again, without having to be told, washed her womb with his seed. The orgasm went on for much longer than the other, but these two insatiable lovers were not quite done with each other.

They spent the better part of the morning and into the afternoon making love until they had to get back to their lives. "I'll see you this evening then, at dinner." She kissed her lover one last time after rushing into her clothes and hurrying down the stairs and out of the old barn that was their favorite meeting place.

"NIALL COME ON, we'll be late." Sonya Davis pushed the diamond stud into her ear as she looked into the mirror and shoved her foot into the high heel stiletto that matched the one she already wore.

She looked at herself one last time, running her hands smoothly down the sides of her short black silk dress that fit her curves like a glove. Niall walked up behind his wife and mirrored the action from behind, only his hands came around and up to cup her breasts as they both looked on in the mirror.

"You look lovely as usual darling. We still have a few minutes." She knew what he was after when he started to lower the straps down her shoulders. "You'll have to make it quick love or we'll be late."

She smiled into the mirror at him as he pushed her forward with her hands planted on the bureau top. He lifted her dress up gently over her ass and pushed the crotch of her panties aside with one hand while fiddling with his zipper with the other.

He led his cock into her sweet opening and slid in, taking that first few seconds to revel in the fact that his sweet young wife still had the hots for him. She never tells him no, no matter how often he asks.

And even though sometimes the stress of work takes it out of him and he's not in the mood, he still thinks their sex life is doing better than most. They had three kids in six years to prove it.

Sonya looked into his eyes in the mirror as he fucked into her from behind, amazed that she can always tell the difference between the two men in her life, that she can keep the two separate. Niall fucks her with short quick jabs; it gets the job done. But nowhere near as well as her lover's much longer and deeper strokes that reaches her very depths.

One supplies the mind-blowing sex and the other the money to keep her in the lifestyle she desired, and she couldn't and wouldn't do without either. "Cum inside me!" Her pussy juiced at the reminder that just this afternoon, a few hour ago, her lover had done the same thing.

"I'm cumming, cumming...!" Niall roared like a bull when he came inside his wife and tugged on her nipples the way he knows she likes. With her panties slipped back in place Sonya fixed herself again before heading down the hallway to say goodnight to her three little darlings, one boy and two girls.

She didn't bother to clean up because she was already making plans for the night to come. She was barely able to contain herself as they walked out the door to the waiting car.

The thought of sitting down to dinner with others, her panties wet as his seed dripped out of her while she looked like the perfectly put together banker's wife had her rubbing her thighs together.

"You seem happy!" Niall lifted her hand to his lips and kissed her fingers as the driver drove them through the streets to the French restaurant they and their friends were about to try for the first time.

"I'm always happy when I'm with you." She leaned over and kissed him, taking it from zero to sixty in a second. She'd have loved to ride his cock in the backseat of their town car but her straitlaced husband would have kittens if she even suggested it.

She's lucky he even still has sex with her after the kids; their sex life had changed drastically once she became a mother.

She'd stopped feeling desirable, stopped feeling like a sexual being and more like a feeding station after each birth. Until she caught the look in her lover's eyes.

She'd been hitting the home gym trying to get her body back in shape and have to admit that she looked better than she did since her early twenties. With her new larger breasts and much tighter ass and neater waist, she knew she turned heads. But it never mattered more than when her lover made notice and started paying more and more attention to her.

They'd been friends for ages, ever since she met him through her best friend. She'd grown up with Valerie here in this small town of Briar Reef, the only time she'd ever been away was when she went away for school.

She'd had wild dreams of moving to the big city, getting a job in the large firm, climbing her way up. That's when she was still the small town innocent, the girl who was willing to work her way up the ladder.

But then she met Niall at a conference her last year in college and all of that changed. He'd offered her a life she could only dream of and she'd jumped at the chance. It helped that she'd found the much older man handsome and exciting.

But all that changed after the babies came. Her exciting and lustful husband had started seeing her as more mother than wife and their love life had tapered off tremendously.

He'd started touching her differently too, and their encounters had become more and more lukewarm, lacking the heat that had been there in the beginning. But then her lover had come along and she once again had a complete and fulfilled life. The best of both worlds.

Niall patted her leg as their lips came apart and sat back in his seat ever the staunch upstanding citizen. They exchanged small talk until the car pulled up in front of the restaurant and the driver let them out.

Dinner was fun, the way it always is when they spend time with their friends. After the dishes were cleared Sonya got up from her seat to head to the lady's room.

"Order me another one darling, I'm going to go call and check on the kids." Two minutes after she left the table her lover's phone rang and he too excused himself from the table.

She was at the sink washing her hands after hanging up the phone when the door squeaked open. She knew it was him when she saw his eyes. "What are you doing in the lady's room lover?"

She walked over to him and ran her finger down his chest. He grabbed her ass in both hands and pulled her in for a tongue-twisting kiss. She pulled her panties off down her legs

"Hurry-hurry, we only have five minutes, I need it so bad." He sat her on the sink in the lady's bathroom and dropped his slacks releasing his cock. "No eat me first." She put her hand on his head, pushing him down, knowing that her pussy was full of cum from earlier.

He licked into her deep loving the taste and smell of her as she held his head in place. Sonya came hard and long on his tongue before he got to his feet and slammed his cock into her.

She closed her eyes in ecstasy as he pounded away at her, her hand wrapped around his neck as they kissed, sharing her taste and his.

CHAPTER 2

"*M*orning Valerie." Valerie O'Rourke waved from her mini convertible coupe as she drove through the little village of Briar Reef, the sunlight glistening off the tresses of her golden blonde hair.

"Morning Dina!" She tooted her horn and called out to a few more people before coming to a stop in the parking lot behind her art gallery. The day promised to be a good one if the number of people she'd seen out and about in the town square was anything to go by.

Of course the holiday weekend would be coming up in a few days and those were always good for business in the past, but with the economy being what it is, there was no guarantee.

She stepped out of the BMW and fiddled with the Hermes silk scarf she had thrown carelessly around her shoulders before tugging on the hem of her skirt to get it back in place.

There were a few more calls of hello and good morning

as she made her way to the shop, and her spirits were lifted. Today is going to be a good day.

SONYA DAVIS PICKED her way over fallen branches, twigs and mountains of dead leaves as she made her way to her secret rendezvous. Leave it to bloody lover boy to call her out here in this mess of a woods. Then again it won't be the worst place they'd ever done it.

Her heart picked up its pace as she got deeper into the dense foliage coming closer to their meeting place. Horny bastard, didn't we fuck just yesterday?

Not that she was going to complain, she loved the fact that her lover was as sex crazed as she was, and since she had nothing to do with her days but wait for the school bus at three, her mornings were all his.

He on the other hand was playing it close. With a business to run and a whole lot of eyes watching his every movement, they had to be careful. But still, none of that stopped her from running when he called.

She didn't notice the climbing heat or the insects that buzzed around her as she walked. She was too busy paying attention to her every step afraid of stepping on one of the confounded traps the hunters like to leave around the place.

As far she knows they've never trapped any other species but man in one of the damn things and she'd have a lot of explaining to do if she got herself snagged in one of the stupid things.

With her head down she didn't see up ahead and that's why the fright was so palpable when she finally did. It was the suddenness you see, coming face to face with her worst nightmare out here alone in the woods.

The scream got trapped in her lungs as she turned in abject horror and ran. Her eyes wide with fright, she hardly saw what was in front of her, her mind filled with the terror behind, and so she didn't see the obstruction that was in her way.

She went flying through the air with a loud scream just as she heard footsteps coming slowly through the brush in her direction, as if someone was coming to her rescue; but by then it was too late.

She landed in the large puddle of water face first and her screams grew more tormented until they were no more. The air was suddenly filled with the stench of burning flesh and the gurgling sound of someone in the final throes of life.

BARNEY DOSS HAD BEEN on one of his usual morning walks through Briar Reef woods when he heard the faint scream coming through the trees. At first he thought it was the sound of a bird, or some other wild animal, but the closer he listened the second time it came, he knew that the sound was more human.

He hasted his step as much as he could with a cane and a bum knee and came up short when he turned the corner and saw the person laying on the ground. "Hey, you okay?"

He hobbled over to the form that wasn't moving, his heart racing in the way anyone's would in a situation like this; alone, in the woods, with people screaming and now one lying still as death on the ground.

"Hey, you there!" There was still no movement from the person who seemed to have fallen, as Barney got closer. "Hey you!" He poked the fallen body in the shoulder with his cane and still there was not a peep.

He was beginning to think the person who he now believed to be a woman had hit her head in the fall and knocked herself unconscious.

"She'll drown herself in that little bit of water for sure." He couldn't bend down because of his knee so he tried rolling her over with the cane. He pushed at her shoulder until he got her moving and stumbled back in horror at the sight that greeted him when he got her face partially lifted before dropping her again.

He fumbled around in his pocket for the mobile phone his granddaughter had got him just the month before but there was no signal. He looked around for help but knew there was none. No one else came here, only him. It had been that way for years now, having the woods all to himself.

The kids had found a better, more exciting place to carry out their misdeeds and the young couples were too busy making a living to have much time for lazy days spent foraging in the woods. While the elderly, had given up on the steep climb up the hill to reach the place.

It was only he Barney Doss who had never given up his love for the deep dark woods where he'd spent many a childhood day. And even with the pain it caused him, he never missed a day come rain or shine. Now his solitude had been disturbed and he doubted he'd ever feel the same way here again.

It took poor old Barney a good half an hour to make it out of the woods and down the hill and then another ten minutes before he came to the O'Rourke farm. He was out of breath and panicked by the time he knocked on the door and then rang the bell.

The housekeeper Mrs. Cline answered on the third hurried knock. "I'm coming, I'm coming, keep your shorts on." Her heavy New England accent came through the thick wood of the door as her footsteps clipped along the marble floor.

She flung the door open to see poor Barney looking as though he was about to keel over. "Why Barney Doss, whatever is the matter with you? Come in, come in." She stepped back to let him enter and he held his hand up to stop her.

"Call the police Eileen, there's a body in the woods. I think someone's been murdered." Her mouth fell open in surprise as she tried to make sense of his words.

"A murder? But there hasn't been a murder here in over fifty years." She felt the way any middle-aged woman without family would at the thought of death. A death so close.

Barney stood in the doorway lacking the strength to lift his foot over the threshold to go inside as Eileen headed for the nearest phone. "Uh police, this is Eileen Cline over at the O'Rourke farm, I have Barney Doss here, he says there's been a murder."

On the other end of the line the surprised desk sergeant asked for more details, which poor Ms. Cline did not have. "Hold on a minute, I'll let him tell you himself." She walked back to the door where Barney was leaning and trying valiantly to catch his breath, and passed him the handheld phone.

"Yes, this is Barney Doss, I was out on one of my morning walks in the woods, looking for birds you see..."

"Yes, yes, but what is this about a murder? Did you see a body?"

14

"Well yes, I was just about to tell you..."

He was cut off by the sergeant once again who asked for the location of the body. It was obvious from the sergeant's tone that he didn't believe it, but he took down the information and went in search of the town's only lead detective.

"Detective Sparks, there's been a call." He passed the paper with the notes he'd taken down to the young woman, who read the note over twice with disbelief.

"Who did you say called this in?"

"Eileen Cline down at the old O'Rourke farm, she says Barney Doss turned up on her doorstep almost half to death and blurted it out to her."

Detective Celia Sparks got up from her chair and grabbed the jacket she'd thrown over the back of it when she came in to work earlier that morning. "Come on Pete we've got a live one." She called out to her junior partner before heading for the door.

"Call the O'Rourke farm, tell Barney Doss not to leave until I've spoken to him. And call the crime scene unit, tell them to meet us there." The situation was so foreign to her that she was sure that she was forgetting something.

Outside she looked up at the sun in the sky and made note of what a perfectly bright and sunny day it was. Certainly not the kind of day one would associate with murder.

She climbed into the driver's seat while her partner officer Bailey got in next to her and strapped in. She gave him a quick rundown and they both looked at each other skeptically neither of them believing for a second that a murder had taken place in heir picturesque little town.

"Are you sure? You know old man Doss is about a hundred if he's a day. Maybe he saw a fallen deer in the

15

distance, or someone taking a nap under a tree or something."

"No one goes there anymore, not since they fixed up the park on the other side of town and I'm sure as old as he is he can tell the difference between a deer and a human."

"Still, murder? Could it be a drunk passed out or something?"

"We'll know when we get there I guess, I'm as flummoxed as you are at the idea."

Detective Sparks didn't say anything more as the car made its way through the center of town and out onto the back roads that would take them to where they were going.

It was a trek getting to the top of the hill and into the woods where they'd been directed but once there, there was no mistaking that it was indeed a murder. Either that or a very unfortunate accident.

"Can you tell who it is?" Officer Bailey asked as he covered his nose from the stench. He'd always admired his superior but had to admit that that admiration went up a notch when she knelt next to the grotesque sight, nose bare and no sign of distaste on her exceptionally beautiful face.

Detective Sparks pulled on her work gloves and tried rifling through the pockets of the deceased but there was no wallet, nothing to give away the identity of the person who now laid at her feet without a face.

"We didn't see a car at the bottom of the hill did we Pete?"

"No, but they could've come in from the other side, why don't I go check?"

"You do that, I'll wait here for the crime scene unit."

Boy were they in for a surprise. There wasn't much that she could do until they got here, and she didn't want to disturb anything more than she already had by rifling through pockets so she stepped back making sure to avoid the bloody liquid that she could see from the fumes still rising from it held some kind of caustic agent.

She stood and looked around at her surroundings. It had been a while since she'd been here herself. Although there wasn't much in the way of crime in the town of just a little bit over three thousand, just the occasional runaway cow, or a cat caught in a tree, she still somehow found her days very well occupied.

There were the calls from the elderly who imagined every sound, every creaking floorboard to be an intruder or a harbinger of imminent death, and those were plentiful.

Or the rare dustup between some tourist and one of the locals who took offense to what they saw as their town being disrespected. That can be for something as simple as spitting chewing gum on the sidewalk.

For all its lack of anything approaching adventure, or even a nightlife, or any of the things a young woman like herself would appreciate for that matter, she loved it here, in this little haven she'd found after working for a few years in the big city.

The move had been a bit of a culture shock for sure in the beginning, and it had taken some time getting used to the change as well as being accepted by the locals who had all been here for generations.

But in the three and a half years that she'd been here the place had grown on her and now she couldn't imagine living anywhere else. Even if she wasn't able to recognize her full potential, there were other things to compensate. Like the peace and quiet that couldn't be bought.

She heard the engine of an approaching vehicle at about the same time she saw officer Bailey huffing his way back up the opposite side of the incline in her direction. "Found it;

you're not going to believe this but that's Sonya Davis, at least it's her car at the bottom of the hill."

"Sonya?" She looked down at the remains and tried to picture the beautiful vivacious woman's face superimposed over what now laid at her feet. She didn't know the other woman personally, they didn't move in the same circles after all. But she knew her enough to say hi in passing.

As a cop she'd been trained to disassociate herself, to separate what she thought she knew of the person from the reality of her cases, but no amount of training can prepare you for something like this. "She was so young." She looked over as the crime scene techs trudged their way over to her side.

She exchanged greetings with Simon Porter the coroner and his crew and they stood around for the first few seconds taking in the unusual sight of a body that had not expired due to natural causes. It was easy to tell from the odd positioning of the body that it was not a natural fall, if the fumes and scent of burnt flesh didn't already give it away.

"A murder it is then." Detective Sparks looked at the coroner after his cryptic comment. "What do you mean?"

"Well, after I got the call and heard all the particulars I thought for sure old Barney's cheese had fallen off his cracker." He popped a handful of peanuts from his pocket into his mouth.

He gestured towards the body with his hand. "But that doesn't look like an accident to me. Not unless she was running with whatever is in that liquid that's giving off that scent and it spilled all over her." He looked around before turning his attention back to her. "I don't see a container."

Detective Sparks nodded her head amazed that for someone who hadn't handled a suspicious death before he sure seemed to be on the ball. "Well, better get to it then, the heat's rising. It's going to be a bitch of a day." She snorted at his irascibleness and stepped back to let him get to work.

For a crew who didn't see many murders, they got right to work, marking off the area, taking samples of the liquid and checking the surrounding area for anything that might shed some light on what had gone on here.

When the coroner finally turned the woman all the way over the severity of her injuries were revealed. There was a lot of indrawn breaths and mutters of disbelief.

"What do you think doc? Is this what killed her, whatever was used to do this to her face?"

"Well, it looks like some kind of acid was used. That in itself might not have killed her outright but the immediate shock to the system might've played a part, not to mention the fact that she was face down in about an inch of liquid."

"This liquid, I know there's some kind of acid in it, but is there any water?" That would mean the difference between an accidental spill of some kind that this poor woman had been unlucky enough to fall into and something more deliberate.

"No, I don't think so. And look at this hole that it's in. This was freshly done in the last day or so. And since we haven't had any rain lately there was no way for water to gather in there unless someone purposely poured it in there."

"Since she was heard screaming just before she was found I guess we can estimate time of death, but you'll check all the same won't you doc?" He touched the back of one of the victim's arms, which was about the only place not affected that was naked to the eye.

"Rigor mortis hasn't begun to set in so the timing sounds about right. Sometime in the last two hours." He fixed his glove with a snap and went back to poking at the body.

JORDAN SILVER

"Hmm, okay doc, I'll leave you to it. Get me what you can as soon as you can." Detective Sparks did her own shaking of the bushes, going back to the car and trying to retrace the steps of the victim. Nothing made sense; there was nothing to give so much as a clue.

"Widen the search Pete, there has got to be something here."

"Yes boss!" They went in two separate directions, taking their time as they made their way deeper into the woods.

CHAPTER 3

Every once in a while Detective Sparks would look back to where the yellow crime scene tape was still visible, trying to get an idea of where the victim had fallen from, though it didn't look like the fall had been a long one. No broken bones that she'd noticed.

But from the way the body had landed it looked almost like she'd been dropped, or thrown through the air. It could almost be mistaken for an accident, just an accidental fall, except for the acid in the water.

Though that too could've been an accident, it didn't ring true, and what are the chances? That would be one hell of a coincidence and she didn't believe in those.

Because she was paying such close attention, looking in the brush and foliage, she didn't miss the trip wire that someone had stretched across the path.

Thinking that this had been deliberate and seeing the evidence of it were two different kettle of fish and so it took a few seconds for her mind to process what it was that she was looking at. This didn't belong here; it wasn't a trap like the one you'd expect to find in the woods. The traps that are illegal for anyone to leave out here since this is public land.

She looked back once again at where the body laid, the body that was still there while the coroner did his job meticulously. She was sure as morbid as it was that he was excited to be handling his first murder.

She also had no doubt the murder will be the talk on everyone's lips for the next little while because he tended to have loose lips. It comes with holding the position he does in the small town.

She looked back and forth between the place where she now stood and the body, guessing correctly that it was the trip wire that had sent poor Mrs. Davis hurtling through the air to land in the little puddle that someone had conveniently left there.

But why had she been coming back this way? Her car had been parked on the other side, so wouldn't she have gone back the way she came? And what was she doing out here alone? Or had she been alone?

She kept moving forward slowly after leaving a little flag to mark the spot where she'd found the wire, eyes peeled to the ground as she heard her partner on the other side of the thick brush across from her, moving through the bushes like a bull in a China shop. She hadn't gone far when she saw the incomprehensible sight of a clown that someone had left nailed to a tree.

At first glance the dummy appeared real, eyes staring straight ahead with what could only be termed as a spooky grin on its face. It was only her training that kept her from crying out or taking a quick step back.

As it is she swallowed deeply and forced herself to keep going before calling out to the others to follow her and warning them to watch their step where she'd left the marker.

"We'll have to take this in as well along with the wire." She ordered the members of the crime scene unit who answered her call.

They both studied the clown dummy looking for any more traps or tricks before it was removed and bagged as evidence, then she checked the surrounding area once again but came up empty.

There was nothing more than the disturbed bushes, no footprints, no snagged pieces of clothing, nothing at all other than the clown and the body to show that anyone other than the victim had been here. Oh and of course the wire.

Could it have been kids fooling around? Had they left the clown here? But why the wire and why the acid in the water? That was taking a joke too far and she didn't know any kid in the area who would do such a thing.

Though she had to look at all the angles she was already quite certain that this was exactly what it looked like, a murder. A very well thought out one too from the looks of it.

Even though she hadn't found anything on her face search she knew it would be careless not to keep looking. In brush this thick there were plenty places to hide stuff. Like the container the acid had come in for instance; that would be helpful. A nice container with lost of fingerprints. If only the murderer would be that accommodating.

They were there for hours cleaning up the scene and making sure they hadn't overlooked anything. The sun was high in the sky by the time she walked back to the car with Officer Bailey at her side.

"What do you make of this? Was it a joke that went too

far? Was someone trying to play one of those pranks you see on television or something do you think?"

"I don't think so Pete, this looks to me like a calculated attack. The only thing I can't figure is what she was doing out here alone."

She could hear the bleating of sheep and the bellowing of cattle off in the distance as they drove back down the hill and along the boundary of the O'Rourke farm, which was the closest home this side of the woods.

She did a quick run through in her head of all the hands who worked there, wondering if it could've been one of them. The problem was at this point it could be anyone.

They were all local boys, men she'd known in one capacity or another since moving here. And though she couldn't picture any one of them being responsible, she knew better than to make that call lightly.

She stopped off at the O'Rourke farm where poor Mr. Doss had been waiting all this time. She knocked as she wiped her feet on the old rustic heavy-duty mat outside the backdoor.

Dogs barked in the distance and the sweet scent of freshly baked pie made its way through the open kitchen window even as the sound of farm machinery reached her ears.

She looked around as far as the eye could see, back up to the woods that bordered one side of the farmland. She'd always liked this place, always found it to be charmingly welcoming. In her mind it was everything that a farm in a small town should be.

The large Grecian columns that lined the front with the extra long porch, black shuttered windows against the starling white of the house, the black roof with three chimneys that she could imagine smoke puffing out of on cold winter nights and the stately trees that graced the huge front lawn. All sat perfectly in the middle of green-green grass.

The place reminded her of the ranch in one of the old nighttime soap opera reruns her grandmother used to watch, Dallas she thinks it was called, but she was too young to remember.

The miles of white ranch fencing, horses grazing off in the distance and the cattle even farther away gave one a feeling of calm and home sweet home. The O'Rourkes owned about five thousand acres of prime land all be told, the richest landowners in town and for miles around.

As large as it was, everything about the place felt cozy, like home. Even the beautifully designed gardens, that ran from beneath the front windows and down the sides of the old Georgian styled house.

And the swing that sat on the marble porch, gave her ideas of idyllic mornings spent wiling away the time in the early sunlight as she drank a cup of coffee and read the paper. Fanciful!

But those were the kind of thoughts that ran through her head whenever she saw the place or came anywhere near it. And no matter how often she saw it, it was always the same.

Though she'd only ever seen it from a distance, or in the magazine she still had at home in her bedside table from the time two years ago when one of the leading house design magazines had done a spread about the place.

Her face heated with a blush when the thought of the owner; Mr. Riley O'Rourke. His family had owned the farm for generations, and he was the first to add onto it, the first to turn it into the moneymaker that it was today.

Just like that soap opera that she could barely remember, he'd found oil, which had immediately taken him from firmly upper middle class to very, very wealthy. So not only was he the best looking man for miles around, he was now the wealthiest, and at one time the most sought after.

This had all been before her time, before she'd moved here. By then he was already married to the beautiful Valerie Troy, the very fashionable, very well learned and well travelled Valerie Troy with her degree in fine arts and elegant airs.

They'd been high school sweethearts, who as the story goes, everyone was sure, would marry and settle down here together. He'd gone to one of the major Ivy League schools as well for his degree in business as was to be expected for someone with his background.

They've been married ten years now, but still no children as yet. Detective Sparks remembered the first time she'd ever laid eyes on Riley O'Rourke in the flesh, the way her heart had skipped a beat; and then the embarrassment when he'd barely spared her a glance.

It was no wonder, even as beautiful as everyone was always telling her she was, she was nowhere near as beautiful as his wife, not even close. And she was lacking all the sophistication of the well-educated cultured girl who'd obviously caught his heart when they were young and still held it in the palm of her hand.

Not that she would've done anything untoward with a married man. She's not that kind of woman; but funny enough, his reaction had made her like him even more. In a town were the whispers about what goes on behind closed doors abound, it was nice to know that there was at least one man who didn't play the field.

The door opened at her third knock, interrupting her thoughts and Eileen Cline, the housekeeper invited her in. "Come in please Detective. Since you're here after all this

A KILLING IN THE WOODS

time I'm guessing old Barney was right, you've found a body. Is it murder then?"

"Thank you Ms. Cline, and yes, there is a body, but the case is still in its early stages yet so we won't know more until we've done a thorough investigation." And if I tell you any more than that I'm sure the whole town will know have heard every word of it before I've driven away from this place.

She was till getting used to the way things worked here in Briar Reef. The grapevine in a small town was almost as effective as the Internet and moved at just about the same speed. And with news of this magnitude she had no doubt that it would be making the rounds long before she got a handle on what was going on herself.

She saw Mr. Doss sitting on a chair at the old woodblock table in the kitchen and made her way over to him. Poor old guy, to think that he'd seen what she had; he must've been horrified to come across a thing like that out there on his own as he was.

"Mr. Doss, I'm going to have an officer take you down to the station to answer some questions, will that be okay?" She wasn't comfortable questioning her only witness here. Unprofessional it may be but she didn't want to be here if Riley O'Rourke or his wife came home.

"But I have to get home, I've been here all morning and..." He sounded a bit flustered and it was obvious that the morning had taken its toll. He was getting up there in age and the sight had been a dreadful one even for someone as seasoned as her.

"I understand that but you're the only witness to a crime.

"But I didn't see anything..." She held up her hand and turned her attention to Ms. Cline who was busy puttering around the kitchen. Not that she wasn't certain the older

27

JORDAN SILVER

woman had already dragged every detail out of him in the time he'd been sitting here waiting.

But there was no help for it, the force was bare skin and bones and she'd needed every hand on the scene, so there was no one to run him down to the station before she could get to him. At least she'd made him stay put until she arrived.

"I'm sorry to impose on you any further Ms. Cline but is it possible we can have somewhere private and out of the way to talk, if you don't mind? I won't be long." The older woman dried her hands on a kitchen towel and smiled at her warmly.

"Why yes of course, come on through here." They followed her into the parlor where Detective Sparks stayed standing while Mr. Doss took a seat in one of the overstuffed chairs.

"Now, Mr. Doss," she pulled the notes the desk sergeant had taken earlier from her pocket. "It says here that you heard the victim scream."

"I did yes, but by the time I got there she was already face down in the little puddle of water."

"What time was this do you remember?" According to the coroner she hadn't been dead for more than an hour by the time we got the first call. But it helped that the old guy was actually there on sight when it happened. Makes things a lot easier.

"I'm not sure," he looked at his watch now as if that would help.

"What time did you leave your house to go on your walk Mr. Doss?"

"Why the same time I leave every morning, a little before eight o'clock. I find that the day isn't as hot at that time."

She looked at the cane he had resting on the chair arm. "You have problems with your legs Mr. Doss?" He rubbed his knee and nodded.

"Been giving me hell for near ten years now give or take. The doctor said a nice walk every so often helps, keeps it from seizing up on me."

"And do you walk there every morning?"

"Just about."

"Do you always take the same path?" He nodded his head as she took down notes. Adding up the time in her head. With his bum knee she figured it would've taken him some time to get over the incline and then into the woods.

"Which side did you come in on?" He gave her the location and she figured she might not be able to get the time exact, but at least she was close enough and his answers jived with what the coroner had said.

"And did you touch the body?"

"Well, I was trying to get her face out of the water there because it looked like she'd knocked herself plumb out, so I poked her with my cane when she didn't answer." He swallowed hard and his hands started to tremble as he remembered what he'd seen.

"And then I saw...what happened to that poor woman? It is a woman isn't it?" Just then Ms. Cline entered the parlor with a tray laden with a pitcher of lemonade, three glasses and a plate of freshly baked cookies.

"How about some nice ice cold lemonade?"

"None for me thanks." Detective Sparks refused. Officer Bailey who had stood quietly by looked at the condensation on the glass jug and swallowed deeply. "I wouldn't mind a glass of that."

She poured him a glass and one for Barney as well and passed out little saucers of cookies. Detective Sparks waited until the room was clear again to continue her questioning, but it didn't take long to figure out she'd gotten all she was going to out of the old man.

"Thank you very much Mr. Doss, if you remember anything else please give me a call. Do you need a lift back to your home?"

"I'd be much obliged young lady." He placed his half empty glass on the side table and wrapped the cookies in a napkin, stuffing them in his pocket.

Officer Bailey wolfed his last one down and emptied his glass while Detective Sparks shook her head. He has the eating habits of a five year old.

"What? I haven't eaten since that egg and cheese sandwich at the station this morning and that was hours ago."

Detective Sparks walked towards the door hurriedly, now in a rush to get away since her job here was done. She'd forgotten about the O'Rourkes while questioning the old man but now she wanted to be gone from her as soon as possible.

She dropped old Mr. Doss off at his door and waited until the old guy made it inside. She'd already put in a full day's work but it was still far from over. Now comes the hard part she thought. Telling the husband that his wife wouldn't be coming home again ever.

CHAPTER 4

Niall Davis was just about to call his wife. He'd been in meetings all morning and hadn't had a chance to check in on her and the kids. It's something he never forgets to do and he was sure she'd be wondering what was keeping him.

"Nancy?" He picked up the phone and spoke to his assistant who sat at a desk just outside the doors to his executive office.

"Yes Mr. Davis?"

"Has my wife called?"

"No sir, she hasn't would you like me to call her now? Oh wait a minute sir."

He heard her greet someone who'd walked into the office. "Sir," she came back on the line, "the police are here, they say they need to speak with you." The police? What could they want?

"Send them in." He hung up the phone and got to his feet as they came through the door, led by his assistant. He came around from behind his desk with his hands in his pockets.

"Hello, what can I do for you? That will be all Nancy." He turned his attention to his assistant who nodded in acknowledgement and left, closing the door behind her.

Detective Sparks had made up her mind on the way up in the elevator that there was only one way to do this. No matter how many times you've done it before, each situation was different, but the end result was always the same, someone's life was going to be devastated.

"Mr. Davis, I'm sorry to have to tell you this, but there's been an accident." She took a deep breath and forged on at the befuddled look on his face. "Your wife was killed earlier this morning." He looked at her with a sort of bemused look on his face not quite registering her words. "I don't understand, what do you mean?"

Niall was fast losing all the feeling in his limbs and it felt like the blood had drained from his brain, leaving him with a feeling of lightheadedness. It had to be a joke, a very sick one, but a joke nonetheless. "I don't think that's funny."

"I'm sorry sir, but it's not a joke. We found your wife's body in the woods outside of town, near the O'Rourke farm."

"In the woods? You're mistaken my wife doesn't go into the woods. She's at home with our children." He reached for the phone and put that call in to his home.

The housekeeper answered on the second ring. "Hello, Davis residence may I help you?"

"Yes, this is Mr. Davis, put my wife on the phone please."

"I'm sorry Mr. Davis, but your wife's not at home."

"Well where is she?" He looked at the cops as the truth began to dawn. This couldn't be; she must be out shopping, Sonya loves to shop.

"I'm not certain sir, she left a little after eight this morning and haven't returned."

"Why that's impossible, she would've told me if she was going to be away from home that long." He hung up the phone without saying anything more and dropped down into his seat.

There was a buzzing in his ear and his limbs felt weak. This couldn't be happening. "How did it...how did she die? Was there some sort of accident?"

"Well sir, the truth is we think she was murdered." His eyes shot up to the detective's in disbelief.

"Murdered? Why that's preposterous."

"That's the way it looks sir. Now I have to ask, where were you between the hours of eight and nine this morning?"

"You think... you can't think that I had anything to do with it."

"We're questioning everyone who knew or was in anyway acquainted with the victim sir." Niall rubbed his hand over his face and tried to get his thoughts in order. "Well I was here of course, same as I always am every morning. I came in at seven thirty on the dot."

"Can anyone vouch for that sir?"

"Well no, I'm always the first one here every morning; no one else gets here until eight thirty."

"Why so early? The bank doesn't open until nine."

"It's the time I've always come in. I like to get a head start on the day."

Detective Sparks took notes while officer Bailey looked around the office. It was a well- appointed room, one of those old world types with the large mahogany desk taking center stage and marble walls and floors.

There was no other decoration in the room except for

the huge potted plant in one corner and a silver framed picture of the family on the desk. Father, mother and three kids all under the age of seven by the looks of it.

A beautiful family, though the wife did look a bit younger than the husband. He was having a hard time comparing the beauty in the photo to the thing they'd picked up off the ground in the woods. Who would want to do a thing like that? His mind went to jealousy; but who and why? Was it a man jealous of his wife having an affair? Or a woman jealous that someone else was having an affair with her husband?

It was too early to tell and there were more questions than answers at this point, but his mind was catching at any and everything, looking for a sign, an opening, anything that would lead them to the bottom of this horrific trail.

"Is there anyone you can think of that might want to hurt your wife sir?" Detective Sparks continued her questioning, though she could already tell that Mr. Davis wasn't going to be of much help. He had the classic signs of someone who was in shock.

"No, no one, everybody liked Sonya." He looked at her without seeing her she was sure, that faraway haunted look in his eyes as he tried to make sense of what she was saying. Although she hated pressuring him in his current state, Detective Sparks carried on, asking all the questions she could think of before closing her little notebook.

"I have to go, I have to see my children. Where is she, where is my wife?"

"The M.E.'s office by now." She looked at her watch. The coroner wasn't qualified to do autopsies in this town so the medical examiner one town over was tasked with doing the autopsies for Briar Reef.

And since this was their first murder in half a century

and a gruesome one at that, she wasn't taking any chances; she wanted everything done by the book. She was sure that as soon as word got out everyone would be looking to her for answers, and she didn't have the first clue where to start.

"I want to see her, are you sure?"

"That's not a very good idea right now sir I'm sorry."

"Why? I thought it was common procedure for the next of kin to identify the body? How can you be sure it's her if..."

"I'm sorry sir, but there was some kind of acid used in the attack."

"Acid? You mean..." He looked as though he'd been poleaxed. "Someone threw acid in my wife's face?"

"We're not at liberty to divulge that information at this time sir."

"So how do you know that it's her? It can be someone else."

"We found her car in the vicinity sir."

She got her phone out and pulled up the picture she'd taken of the victim's hand with her wedding ring. She'd been very careful not to include anything else in this particular photo.

"Do you recognize these sir?" He stared in horror at the image as if the truth was finally settling in. "Yes, they're hers. They belonged to my grandmother." He stared at the picture of the rings he'd put on his wife's hands all those years ago, still not quite believing that this was real

"I'm very sorry for your loss sir."

"I don't...I don't understand, how could this happen?" He looked back and forth between the two of them hoping for something, anything that would make sense of this madness. But all he saw on their faces was pity.

"Do you have any business rivals sir? Anyone you think

might hold a grudge for some imagined slight?" He was shaking his head before she was through asking.

She didn't really believe that that was the case but she had to ask since she had nothing else to go on, and sometimes it was the one thing you overlooked that held the key in a case like this.

She'd learned long ago to always expect the unexpected, and to never take anything for granted. Besides, this early in the case, everyone was a suspect until they were cleared of suspicion by process of elimination.

"No, no one. Sonya and I were very private people, we kept mostly to ourselves except for the time we spent with our friends the O'Rourke s." There goes that name again she thought as she made note of that.

"As to my business, of course not. We're a bank; we might get the odd recalcitrant customer every now and then. Someone upset that we'd turned them down for a loan. But no one that would go to these extremes. Please, can't you tell me what happened to my wife?"

She was moved by the real pain in his voice but it would be the epitome of unprofessionalism to divulge that information at this point. She'd already slipped up enough by mentioning the acid. Thank heaven he'd let it drop or she'd have had a lot of explaining to do if word got back to her superiors.

"Thank you for your time sir, we'll be in touch when we know anything else or if there's any more questions." She wanted to leave to give him some privacy as it looked like he was about to break. "Is there someone we can call for you?" He shook his head and slumped back in his chair looking utterly defeated.

This wasn't her first time paying this kind of call, informing someone that their loved one had died or been

36

murdered. But it was the first since she moved to the small town. It didn't get any easier with time.

She was dead tired by the time she walked out of his office and out onto the street. Both physically and emotionally drained. It was almost three thirty by the time they got back to the station house and there was still tons of work to be done.

She looked over her notes at her desk as she ate a stale tuna salad sandwich from the deli at the grocery store and took sips from her bottle of lukewarm water. "Pete, did you get that list of people I asked you for?"

"Yes I did boss." He tore off a sheet of paper from his notebook and walked over to drop it on her desk. "That's it? Just the O'Rourkes, the housekeeper and the nanny?" She looked up at him skeptically.

"All I came up with so far. It seems the lady was a very private person just like her husband said. If she hung around with anyone else no one knew. Other than her charity and her husband's partners at the bank there doesn't seem to be anyone who she was close to." He shrugged and walked back to his desk across from hers.

She looked down at the piece of paper again, thinking how sad it was if this were true. The woman she'd seen out and about town seemed like someone who'd been surrounded by friends and admiring people.

Even she had more friends and acquaintances than could fit in a thimble. "There's no way this is it, but I guess it's a good place to start." She threw the rest of her unwanted sandwich in the trashcan beneath her desk and pushed her chair back to stand.

"Aw, what now? We just got..." He stopped belly aching at her glare. She guessed it was easy to understand his lackadaisical attitude seeing as this was the first murder investigation he would be working on. But she'd trained him well enough to know that he'd get the job done.

She was back on the street half an hour later, headed back out to the farm to question Mr. and Mrs. O'Rourke about the death of their friend. She'd already heard a few whispers just in the station house but she was sure the news would be all over town by sundown.

"I called the M.E. Pete, he won't have anything for us until tomorrow but he did say it was hydrofluoric acid, a very strong concentration. It was that that he thinks caused a pulmonary edema."

"A what now?"

"Plainly speaking it's an excess of fluid in the lungs, but the thing is, you can buy this acid from any hardware store and it's regularly used for household cleaning, in weaker concentrations of course. I'll need you to get on that right away. Go around to all the local hardware stores here, and a couple of the surrounding towns."

"And what will you be doing?"

"I'm heading back out to the farm to question Mr. and Mrs. O'Rourke, see if I can get some idea of who she may have known that's not written down on that piece of paper. But first I think I should drop in at the Davis home and have a talk with the housekeeper and the nanny."

She popped a piece of gum in her mouth and chewed as she headed to her police issue vehicle while officer Bailey headed to another that they kept in reserve. She wondered if the thing would even start as she put her car in gear and headed back out of town.

THE DAVISES LIVED in an upscale part of town about a half

an hour away from the O'Rourke farm. Their home was no less grand, another eighteenth century Georgian home, this one white with green shutters sitting on about three acres of land that was mostly lawn with a little manmade lake in the back.

Homes here could go for millions and were in high demand from out-of-towners looking for a change of life. She'd already done a run on their finances and was waiting for the information to come in, but so far there were no alarm bells ringing there.

As she exited the car she went over her earlier interview with the husband, trying to remember if there was anything he'd given away in his behavior but she hadn't picked up anything from him, nothing of note anyway.

On her way out, she'd asked his assistant if he'd been there in the office when she clocked in this morning, and the woman had confirmed his claim that he showed up to work at the same time like clock work every day.

She closed the car door and made her way to the front door and rang the bell. She could hear voices coming from inside and came up short when the door was opened by the housekeeper and she saw the O'Rourke s sitting in the den with the bereaved husband.

He looked destroyed, that was the only word for it. If he was the one responsible he was a damn good actor. She fancies herself a very good judge of character; something that came in handy in her line of work, and unlike what's popularly thought the husband didn't seem like the culprit.

But it was too early to tell, so she didn't let herself get tunnel vision. "Good evening everyone, it's good that you're here Mr. and Mrs. O'Rourke I was coming out to see you next. Mr. Davis I wonder if I may see your housekeeper and nanny?"

He gestured with the glass of amber liquid in his hand down the hallway where the woman she assumed was the housekeeper had just disappeared after letting her in. "You'll find Nettie in the kitchen and Bridgette will be upstairs in the nursery with the kids."

"Thank you!" She headed towards the kitchen looking at the family photos that lined one wall of the hallway on the way there. They looked like a happy family in every one, but she knew very well how people could hide their true inner feelings from the world. She'd been doing it for years. Hiding her discontent with life.

"Hello, Nettie is it? I was wondering if you could answer some questions for me."

"Sure, but I'm in the middle of getting dinner started." The older woman continued bustling around the kitchen going from the refrigerator to the stove and back before going to the island to chop vegetables.

"Why don't you sit down Detective? Would you like something to drink, some water, a soda?"

"No thanks. So what time would you say Mrs. Davis left the house this morning?"

"About eight or a little before I think! Mr. Davis hadn't been gone long, maybe a half an hour or so I think, his usual time."

"And did she usually leave the house this early?"

"Not usually no, but lately..." She chopped into a carrot rather viciously, so hard that the sound echoed around the room.

"But lately what?"

"Lately she's been acting strange. Leaving the house at all hours, sometimes at the drop of a hat. She'd get a phone call sometimes and just drop everything and go."

"How long has this been going on?" She stopped with

the knife in her hand and looked up to the ceiling. "I'd say it all started about a year and a half ago, but here lately it got worst."

"And she never told you where she was going?"

"Why would she? I'm just the housekeeper."

"And what time do you come in to work?"

"I live in, in the carriage house over the garage." She pointed with her knife out the window. "I'm here by six every morning rain or shine." She went back to her chopping with a look on her face that said she was not enjoying this in the least.

"And what was their relationship like?"

"Happy as anyone I guess. They have their rows like any married couple, nothing too alarming. He's never hit her if that's what you're getting at. He..." Her voice was testy, defensive even and Detective Sparks took note of it.

"I'm not accusing anyone Ms. Nettie, just trying to get a picture that's all." Nettie went back to her chopping with less force this time and a slight blush as if only now realizing that she'd overreacted to the question.

"So you say she changed in the last year and a half. How about him, did he change in anyway that you've noticed?" She shrugged her shoulders.

"Mr. Niall works very hard, it's understandable if he has an off day here and there."

"In what way do you mean?"

"Well, after the babies came so close together, it was a bit chaotic around here. Even with the nanny they're a handful. Mr. Davis would sometimes wander off by himself, but then again she'd wander off herself sometimes too like I said."

"And where did they go in these wanderings?"

"I wouldn't know and it wasn't my place to ask.' She stopped and gazed off into space for a second as if recalling something of import before going back to her chopping again.

"I did notice that she was a lot happier lately, in and out of the house more and more often, but she was always here when he came home in the evenings." It was obvious that the elderly woman did not approve.

It was sounding more and more like Sonya Davis had indeed been having an affair, but it was too early to tell yet. Still, it was a place to start. "Did you like her Ms. Nettie?" The knife stopped mid slice and the older woman looked at her a bit miffed.

"Why what a question to ask. Of course I liked her, in my own way. But I don't need to-to do my job now do I."

"And where were you between the hours of eight and nine this morning Ms. Nettie?"

"I was here, where I always am." She stomped over to the stove and added a handful of vegetables to the stew she had going on the stove.

"One more question; how long have you worked for the Davises?"

"I raised Mr. Niall when he was a boy and then I came here when he got married to look after the house and his family."

"Okay, that's all for now, can you direct me to the nursery please?" She pointed with her knife. "Up the stairs, first door on the right, next to the master bedroom." Detective Sparks turned and left the room, stopping in the doorway to look back at the other woman who had gone back to her stirring.

"I might have some more questions for you later, give me a call if you think of anything that might help." She passed one of her cards to the woman who shoved it in her apron pocket.

CHAPTER 5

*D*etective Sparks made her way up the stairs and heard the children at play. She cleared her throat to announce her presence and the other woman looked up at her entrance. The young nanny looked just as she'd expected, a brown haired Irish lass with light green eyes.

"Hello!" Her Irish accent was thick, her smile charming and Detective Sparks wondered at the folly of women who hire women like that to live in their house with their husbands and children.

Not that she thought all pretty young girls had ulterior motives, but just one look and she was already picking up on the fact that this one at least, was a lot more than she seemed.

Maybe it was the New Yorker in her that made her so cynical but whatever it was, her senses were already on high alert. All the same, she knew better than to pass judgment on someone just based on gut instinct alone.

"Hello, Bridgette, I'm Detective Sparks I'm here to ask

you some questions about Mrs. Davis." The nanny looked down at the children, a boy of about six and two girls four and two or almost two. "May we step outside please?"

Detective Sparks stepped aside to the let the other woman pass and followed her across the hall to what turned out to be the nanny's room. The room was bare and about what you'd expect someone who was living and working in someone else's house to be.

There was one lone picture on the nightstand of Bridgette and an older man and woman, probably her parents. On the bureau there was a comb and brush set, a few hair baubles and some bottles of perfume. The room was neat, nothing out of place and she was dressed in a light green skirt that came down below her knees and a white peasant blouse.

Nothing too revealing, but then she didn't need much to enhance her beauty. "You say you're here about Mrs. Davis, such a horrible thing. The poor little ones, I don't think they quite understand, maybe Junior a little bit, but his sisters..."

Her voice tapered off as she sat on the edge of her bed. "I don't know what I can tell you, I wasn't privy to Mrs. Davis' private life."

"How long have you worked for the family?"

"Let's see, I came when Junior was about two, just before little Teresa was born,"

"And who took care of Junior before that?"

"Why Nettie of course. But Mrs. Davis thought she was too old to take care of two children and so they hired me."

"And how did you hear about the job?"

"They advertised in the paper of course."

"And where did you live before that?"

"I came over from Ireland, this was my first time in America."

"Do you have family here, know anyone else other than the Davises?"

She reddened and clasped her hands between her knees. "Well there is Riley and his wife." Detective Sparks looked at her when she mentioned his name, it was the way she said it, the secret little smile on her face.

"And how well do you know the O'Rourkes?"

"Not that well I guess, I just see them when they're here. He's very nice, he comes more often than she does; he likes to be with the children." Odd but not necessarily suspicious!

"How often would you say he came to the house without his wife?" Bridgette shrugged her shoulders and rested back on her palms, pressing her breasts taut against the cotton of her shirt and revealing the fact that she wasn't wearing a bra.

"Maybe twice a week, sometimes more. He likes to play with the children."

"And what was their relationship like? Mrs. Davis and Mr. O'Rourke I mean."

"He's a very handsome man don't you think?"

Yes, yes I do! She didn't say the words out loud of course, just left the question hanging in the air between them. "Well?"

"They were friends, very close friends. She was always happiest when Mr. Riley was around."

"And her husband? How was she with him?"

"Normal I guess, like any other couple. They had their fights just like anyone."

"About what?"

"You know, the usual, about the children, life, they were always arguing about something lately."

"What about specifically do you know?"

"I guess it was about the way she'd disappear without

telling anyone where she was running off to." Detective Sparks made note of that, but vividly remembered Niall Davis saying that his wife would never leave the house for any length of time without first letting him know.

Now here was the housekeeper and the nanny both claiming different. Could it be that he didn't know, that he had no idea...but wait, she just said they'd argued about it.

"Where did she go do you know?"

"No idea, but it was very suspicious. I think he suspected her of having an affair."

"Did you hear him say that?"

"Not in so many words, no, but it was easy to read between the lines."

Her mind was already going in that direction but she needed more to go on. Seems to be the theme of the day. "Would you know of any places she liked to hang out? Did she go out late at night?"

"Not usually no, and not without him. He kept a very close watch on her when he was home. I don't think they went out much, and it was always with the O'Rourke s when they did."

Again the way she said this was very leading and Detective Sparks wondered if she was trying to tell her something in a roundabout way. "And where were you this morning between the hours of eight and nine?"

"I was here of course. I get up at six every morning with the kids."

"And Mrs. Davis, what time did she get up?" Bridgette twisted her brow and gave the question some thought.

"I'd have to say just a bit after seven, yes, Mr. Niall had just gone out the door when she came down. I was getting the children's breakfast ready."

"And what did she do when she came down?"

"She asked Nettie for her morning coffee and then the phone rang."

"Which phone, the house phone or her cell?"

"No it wasn't a ring, I remember now, it was a text message."

The victim's phone had been found in her jeans pocket and was down at the station in the evidence room waiting for tech to go through it. It was pass coded so Detective Sparks hadn't been able to go through it as yet. But this information was very helpful.

They'd gone through her car but there was nothing there of any use to the investigation. Nothing to point them in the direction of who, she might have met. "So what happened after she got the text? Did she answer do you know?"

"I'm not sure, I just know she ran back up the stairs and took a quick shower before running out the door."

"So she got a text not long after her husband left but you don't know from whom."

"No, I don't know. Maybe you should ask Mr. and Mrs. O'Rourke , they were very close." Again with the innuendos!

"Okay, thank you for your time, I won't keep you away from the kids any longer. Here's my card, give me a call if you think of anything else." She left her to go back to the kids who were busy playing with their toys and headed back downstairs to the den where she found Mr. Davis sitting alone with his head hanging down.

"Oh Mr. Davis, where did the O'Rourke s go? I need to talk to them."

"Valerie was very upset so she asked Riley to take her home. They were very close you know, they went to school together."

He took a sip from his glass and rested back in the chair.

She thought in that moment that she'd be very surprised if he had anything to do with his wife's death, he looked like a very broken man.

"Okay then, I guess I'll head out to the farm."

"Have you found anything? Anything at all you can tell me?"

"Not as yet sir, we're still gathering all the evidence. Is there someone you can call to come..."

"No, there's no one, no one now."

She said her goodbyes and headed out the door and into the cooling evening. The sun was already going down in the late summer sky as she made her way back to the car. She put a call in to officer Bailey to see if he'd learned anything helpful.

"What have you got for me Pete?"

"Well, it's like looking for a needle in a haystack isn't it. You'd be surprised how many people buy this stuff. I've got all the credit card purchases from the last month, and some of the stores had working cameras but not all. I'm collecting all the information now and heading back that way."

"Go home once you've logged it in."

"What about you?"

"Me, I have one more stop to make and then I'm packing it in unless something else comes up."

"Okay, did you get anything?"

"Not as yet no, I'll go back over my notes tonight."

She hung up and put a call in to tech to see if they were getting anywhere with the phone. "It's encrypted, I don't know many people who do this with their personal phones but there you have it. I'll crack it yet don't you worry."

"Let me know as soon as." She hung up the phone and pulled out onto the street. She should've known it wouldn't be that easy, but she was sure that text was the answer to the whole thing. Whoever had been on the other end of it, had to know something about where Mrs. Davis was going when she left the house this morning.

She went over all that she'd learned so far and tried to get a picture in her head. She gets a text, takes a rushed shower and leave less than an hour after her husband went off to work.

She went to the woods, the isolated woods. A place where not that many people go any longer!

Was it an assignation? Had she been there before? There was nothing there to suggest it, but why the woods?

Did she think someone was in trouble? If so who? There were too many variables, too many angles. She needed more for that picture to become clearer.

What was she wearing? Had she been dressed for a romantic tryst? Jeans and some kind of tank top she was certain but couldn't swear to it because the acid had eaten away most of it along with the victim's chest.

She closed her eyes for a quick second when she came to a red light and brought the crime scene back into focus. She'd still been wearing her wedding ring. Do women wear their wedding rings when going to meet their lover?

And the clown, why was it there? She believed too that that had to play a very big part in the whole mess. But why? Sure there'd been a spate of clown sightings all over the country in the last year. Some sort of promotion for an upcoming horror film she was told. But nothing like that had ever happened here until now.

On a whim she picked up her phone and called Mr. Davis. He answered on the third ring, his voice thick with unshed tears. "Yes, hello, who is this?"

"Sir, this is Detective Sparks, sorry to bother you.

"Yes, what is it?"

49

"I was wondering sir, did your wife like clowns?"

"Why do you ask?"

"Just something that would help with the investigation.

"I don't see how... no, no she didn't. In fact, she was terrified of them." Her heart tripped in the way it always does when she'd found something, something important.

"And who else knew this sir, apart from you?"

"Well, I'm not very sure; I don't think she went around advertising it. What is this about?"

"Thank you very much for your time sir. I'll be in touch." She rung off and tapped her fingers on the steering wheel as she made the turn that would take her off of the main road and onto the track that lead out to the O'Rourke farm.

CHAPTER 6

The farm was no less beautiful in the setting sun that it had been earlier this afternoon. She could see it from a different angle this time and noted that it was a shorter and more direct drive coming from the Davis estate. Unless of course your aim was a secret hideaway closer to the woods. 'Don't go there Celia' she chided herself.

If Sonya Davis were having an affair with Riley O'Rourke, would she have gone to all that trouble to go into the woods? There were more than enough places scattered around the farm to go to if that were the case. And more comfortable too no doubt.

They hadn't found any soiled mattresses hidden away, or a tent set up for secret trysts; nothing that would lead anyone to suspect someone was having sex out there. Not even an indentation in the grass. Surely they would've left some kind of evidence behind if this is something that had been going on for a while.

Her eyes searched out the landscape; she could see silos,

barns, some of them older and probably not in use. And she remembered that when she was here earlier the farm hands had been nowhere to be seen.

Which meant that there were plenty of places between the house and the workers where lovers could've met without anyone being the wiser, if they were careful. But why would a lover play such a dirty trick with the clown?

As she drove along the white ranch style fence that circled around the twenty or so acres where the house sat, she saw a lone figure walking back towards the house. From the way her stupid heart reacted she was sure it had to be him. And she still had no answers as to why he effected her like this, even after all this time.

It's not like he was the first good-looking guy she'd ever met. Granted, he was way ahead of the others, but still. And she wasn't at all the kind of woman who'd go after a married man. Not that he'd ever given her the time of day. He probably didn't even know that she existed, or so she told herself.

But somehow whenever she saw him, or even thought of him, she had the same reaction; it was uncanny. She'd moved here from the big city to get away from an unrequited love that had got out of hand.

She shivered at the reminder of the upheaval in her life and all that had gone on before she made the move to this place. She'd had no intentions on spending her life in what she once saw as a backwoods town with a population of three thousand.

No, she was more comfortable in the bustling metropolis that had been home her whole life. But when her stalker had infiltrated her life in every possible way, making it so far as into her bedroom in the middle of the night while she slept, she'd decided it was time for a change.

After the trial when he'd gotten away with little more

than a slap on the wrist after tormenting her for more than a year, she'd been disgusted with the whole system. The system that she'd worked so hard for had let her down and she'd started seeing herself in all the women who needed her help afterwards.

She was close to throwing in the towel though she'd never quit at anything in her life, but feeling the way she did, she saw no other way. It was hard looking in those women's faces and giving them the same old bullshit line now that she knew the truth firsthand.

Her captain had seen the cracks and came to the rescue. He'd grown up here in this small town well off the beaten path and instead of letting her give up on her life's work, had talked her into giving this place a try, at least for a little while.

He'd put in a good word for her with the mayor and since the town was about to lose its only senior investigator who'd been on the job for the better part of thirty years and was on his way out she'd jumped at the chance.

It was a steep contrast from what she was accustomed to, but she'd found her footing here and the place had grown on her. All had gone smoothly with the transition except for this one pesky matter. Her attraction to the town's wealthiest man.

It would've been easier if it were his money she was attracted to. At least that she could fight against and stand a better chance at winning. But this attraction ran much deeper and was a source of discomfort whenever their paths crossed, which thankfully wasn't that often.

Riley heard the engine coming down the lane, towards the house and turned at the back door where he was just about to wipe his feet on the welcome mat. "Dammit!" He took his hand away from the doorknob and walked back down the steps.

He stood with his arms folded and waited for the driver to get out after coming to a stop. He should've known it would be her after seeing her at the house earlier. "Good evening detective." He took her in-in one glance then looked away.

"Good evening Mr. O'Rourke I wondered if I could ask you and your wife some questions."

"You can ask me and you can do it out here. My wife's in bed." He could see the question in her eyes. It was still quite early in the evening and no one went to bed at this hour, not even in their sleepy little town.

"She was very upset so I gave her something to help her sleep. Now what can I do for you detective?" She didn't know how to take his words, why would he put his wife to bed this early?

He had to know that the police would want to have a word with her since she and the victim had been such close friends. And hadn't she told them both that she was coming to see them when she got done with Mr. Davis?

First they left the Davis residence and now this. "I would've liked to speak to both of you but I guess I can speak to your wife some other time." She closed the door with a little more force than was necessary and walked over to stand in front of him. He towered over her by a good few inches and she hoped that he couldn't see the pulse racing in her throat, or hear the way her breath hitched at his nearness.

She felt just a little annoyed and had to clear her throat twice before she could get the words past the sudden lump in her throat. "So, how well did you know the deceased?"

She got out her trusty little notebook not quite sure why she was so upset with him all of a sudden.

"I knew her very well, as well as I knew her husband." She listened closely for any inflection in his voice.

"I've been told that you spent a lot of time at the Davis residence while Mr. Davis was away from home. Can you tell me what..."

"I like the Davis children. Sonya suffered a bit of post-partum depression after Abigail was born." Oho, touched a nerve have I? She thought as she took a quick look at him before looking back down at her notes.

"Abigail, would that be the youngest Davis child?"

"Yes, as I was saying, she didn't handle it very well, giving birth to another child so soon after Andrea was born so I went over there sometimes to help out."

"That seems a bit strange doesn't it? A man with all you have to do here, why did you make the effort? Where did you find the time?" From the look he gave her he was obviously not too pleased with her line of questioning but it couldn't be helped. She had a job to do and beating around the bush or showing any type of preferential treatment was out of the question.

"Because her husband was busy at the bank and my wife had her art gallery to see to. I was the only one who had any free time throughout the day to see to her. We were friends, and whatever you or anyone else may think, that's all it was."

Did he seem a bit defensive? "When you say what anyone else might think, have there been talk?" Now she looked at him head on, hoping to read the truth in his eyes.

"No, there was never any talk." Not until today anyway Riley thought silently.

It was something his own wife had hinted at, well not so

much hinted, but he'd read between the lines of her words and didn't like what he came away with. He didn't even know where it was coming from, and why now. She'd never had a problem with their closeness before, his and Sonya's.

She'd never seemed threatened by it and he'd never given her reason to. Or maybe it had been there all along, her distrust, and he'd been too blind to see it. And now here was someone else hinting at the distasteful suggestion.

"Any more questions detective?"

"Well yes, when was the last time you saw the deceased?"

"I saw her last night, we had dinner together." Detective Sparks swallowed hard and looked down at her notebook.

"We were joined by my wife and her husband." He gritted the words out through clenched teeth.

"And how did she seem to you?" She hated that she felt such relief at his words and did her best to hide it.

"The same as always. Bright, vivacious, fun. And before you ask, I didn't see her this morning and I wasn't out in the woods. Neither do I know what she was doing in there."

He ran his hand over his wild mane of jet-black curls in frustration. It was still hard for him to accept that the woman he'd seen just the night before across the dinner table, the woman he'd spent so many hours laughing and joking with, was actually gone.

He knew the cop had a job to do, but he wished her to hell all the same. And why do all their questions have to sound so accusatory? There were things that a person didn't want to and shouldn't have to share with outsiders, did that make them suspicious?

He, his wife, and the Davises had been close for years. It's true that he and Sonya had become closer in the last year and a half but so what. Is that a crime? Now his own wife was upset to the point that he had to tranquilize her and this woman was on his doorstep looking at him with suspicion in her eyes.

"Have you been in the woods at all lately Mr. O'Rourke?"

"No, not since I was a kid. I have better things to do with my time. If I need to take a walk I have more than enough land to do that on. Now if there's nothing else, I need to get back to my wife."

He turned and walked away, leaving her stymied by his hostility. Could there be something to what the nanny intimated? And her own growing suspicions? And what about that statement he made? Whatever anyone might think? Who, who was thinking that he'd had an affair with the dead Mrs. Davis?

She looked up at the house before turning and going back to the car. She needed to speak to Mrs. O'Rourke now more than ever but it looked like that was going to have to wait. Tomorrow, she'd go see the other woman at the gallery first thing in the morning.

She drove back down the lane, her mind in turmoil. She knew better than to let her emotions play a part in an investigation but she couldn't help but be disappointed. Though it was still too soon to tell, if she were looking in from the outside she'd have to say that so far he was the only one that stood out.

She didn't go back to the station but headed home to the little cottage she'd rented in the heart of town. She'd got the place for a song, at least a third of what she would've paid for the same kind of accommodations in the city.

The place was neat and out of the way with its little garden out back and the trees that shielded it from view of anyone driving by. She'd been lucky to find it or more to the point that the captain had found it for her just when she needed it.

The owners had moved away after spending their lives here. Gone to some retirement home in Florida where they were enjoying sun and surf. They'd left all the furniture and she hadn't needed to change a thing, except the mattress since she was never one for home decor.

Though the place looked like something out of a nine-teenth century inn, it did fit with the general ambience of Briar Reef so she saw no need to fiddle with it. Plus it had saved her from having to shell out thousands of dollars.

She used one of the spare bedrooms as an office and that's where she headed now. She dropped her bag on the chair behind the desk and headed back out to the kitchen to find something to eat when her stomach growled a reminder that she hadn't eaten since the few nibbles she'd taken of the stale tuna fish sandwich at lunch.

She put on the kettle to make herself a cup of tea as she foraged in the refrigerator for leftovers. She had some nice pasta from the only Italian restaurant for miles and a couple slices of cold cheese pizza. Neither of which interested her.

It was finally setting in that she had her first murder case in years, and the first on which she was the lead. She called to mind everything that she'd learned about handling a case like this, but there was one blaring difference. Briar Reef is astronomically different from New York.

She couldn't see handling the local residents of the small town she now called home the same way she'd done with the denizens of one of the largest cities in the country. As much as she hated the idea, she knew she'd have to handle everyone with kid gloves.

She was astutely aware that this was also a first for many of them. And since the last murder had been a domestic situation, which had been very cut and dry and rather isolated, she knew that there would be fear amongst the residents here if she didn't get a handle on things soon.

She settled for some toast and a cup of her favorite jasmine tea before heading back to her home office to get down to work. The way things were looking she was sure she'd be here for a while, that her days and nights will be long until she solved this thing.

As she poured over her notes, she realized that her mind kept coming back to Riley and their strange exchange. All the questions in her mind seemed to be centered around him, something she knew could become a problem if she let it.

She tapped her pen against the desk as she looked out the window at the darkening sky. Outside everything seemed still, a slight contrast to the morning and she wondered what the next day would bring.

She thought of Mr. Davis who was going to bed tonight without his beautiful wife beside him, and those three young children who were now left without a mother. And she thought of Sonya Davis and what had been done to her. This last thought brought her mind back in focus and she settled down to work.

CHAPTER 7

By nightfall the news had spread all around town and everyone had their own opinion as to what had taken place. In the local pub where most of the patrons who liked to imbibe on the odd weekend gathered, it was all anyone could talk about. Suggestions were made and theories bandied about, and rumors and whispers of rumors were started.

Officer Pete Bailey took up his usual seat at the small bar and perused the room where other patrons were seated at small wooden tables with mugs of their favorite brew, some long forgotten in favor of the latest gossip.

In the background some soft unrecognizable melody piped through the outdated speaker system as voices spoke in hushed tones as everyone tried to come to terms with a murder in their town.

For some it was a first, since they hadn't been born when the last one occurred, and their innate fear of being murdered in their sleep was heavily mixed with the excitement of the movie like scenario, as the story grew more embellished with each telling.

"It was old man Doss who found her I heard. Sad thing, very sad thing. Such a young woman." Sam Fields the owner of the feed store and was one of the few there who was around for the old case, tipped his bottle of brew to his head after making that announcement to his table of interested cohorts.

Nigel Thorne and Gary Wesley, who both worked for the post office were joined by Elijah Stone who owned the town's only auto repair shop. These four along with Sam made up one group while at another table, Jeffrey Spooner, the grocery owner and his wife Sophia, sat with their heads together.

All over the usually lively room people were more reserved, whether from fear of the unknown or because of the respect most humans have for death, when they feel their own mortality staring them in the face, it was not known.

"So what gives Pete? Any news on what went on here?"

"Now Sam, you know I can't discuss that with you."

"Well can you at least tell us how she died? I hear tell that her face was gone, is that true?"

Pete could've done without that reminder. He'd spent the better part of the day trying to get that image out of his head. With all the running around he'd done today he was able for pockets of time to put it out of his mind, but once his mind stopped running it always came back to that atrocity, something he was sure he had to look forward to for a long time to come.

That's why he was here on a weeknight when he usually only came in every once in a while on the weekend. Those images had ran him out of his home where there was nothing but four walls and empty rooms, and those dreadful images to keep him company.

He should've known there would be no escaping it though. That in a town like theirs it would be the talk on everyone's tongue. He was still coming to terms with the horror himself and though he'd bemoaned the fact from time to time that his job was little more than helping little old ladies and men to cross Main Street, he wished he could go back to yesterday.

Yesterday when the most pressing thing he had to look forward to was whether or not he'd be able to get the time off to take his mama to her doctor's appointment next week.

A day when there was nothing as horrid as murder to taint the beauty he'd always enjoyed since his childhood days in this serene village that time had long overlooked.

A day when he sat out on a park bench and watched the local kids at play, knowing that they were safe unlike their counterparts in the big city. Now that was all gone and even those kids he was sure, will be touched by this event that was bound to change the landscape of their sleepy little town.

"Like I said Sam, I can't discuss it."

"I expect Detective Sparks knows what she's doing." Just then his phone rang and he saw that it was Celia, Detective Sparks. There was a time when he'd see that number on his phone and his heart would give a little blip.

Ever since she showed up here when he was a young lad, fresh out of the academy he was star struck. Still is for that matter. It didn't take long to know that she knew what she was doing even though she was never really given the opportunity to show off those skills that she'd learned back where she came from.

He'd been instantly attracted, to her mind, the person

she was; but it was her beauty that had held him spellbound for the better part of three years. She sure didn't look like anyone else in town, or anyone he'd have expected to find on the force.

Her dark tresses and those bright blue eyes, not to mention her slender statuesque form looked more suited to a Paris runway than hidden away here in this out of the way place where no one ever hardly came.

He imagined most people felt the same way. He'd seen the men of the town's reaction to her in those first days. Had seen her work hard to overcome their disbelief that she was capable of the job she'd been hired to do.

And the women, who'd looked at her askance as was to be expected in a small town like this where everyone practically lived on top of each other. But she'd proven herself many times over, overcoming what he now saw as their prejudice against a pretty face.

It had taken him much longer and truth be told he still wasn't all the way over what it is that he felt for her, but he'd learned to live with it; this unrequited love or lust whatever you want to call it.

He'd never done anything as crass or stupid as to approach her with his budding feelings, but it had been hell working so close to her, sitting in the office at the desk across from hers day in and day out with that beauty staring him in the face.

"Yes boss?"

"Just got a call that there're some kids up in the woods disturbing the scene."

"Why don't you call patrol to go take a look?"

"Already did, but I wanted to head back up there anyway."

He looked towards the window and out into the night

where it was now full dark. "I'll meet you there." He hung up and put his empty bottle down on the bar. "I'll see you guys later."

"Trouble?" He didn't bother answering Sam's question as he headed out the door.

$$\sim$$

DETECTIVE SPARKS LEFT her house at about the same time and headed for her old beat up truck that she'd bought off of old man Stevens. She didn't need much more than that to get around since most places were within walking distance.

She could've taken the police issue vehicle but since it was late and she knew from this morning that her old beater could handle the terrain much better she decided to forego it.

Riley O'Rourke had been the one to call in to the station when he saw the strange light in the trees in the woods behind his place. The call came just in time to save her from herself since she'd just been sitting there making herself crazy with her thoughts.

She knew that time was running out for them, that the first twenty-four to forty-eight hours made all the difference in the world when it came to a murder case, but she just wasn't getting it. And the fact that her mind kept coming back to Mr. O'Rourke wasn't helping matters.

She hated to admit it, but he was looking more and more like the guilty party; something she knew was dangerous because there was no outward sign that he was. Maybe it was because she wanted so much for him not to be part of it that was making her even more suspicious.

She drove through the night and parked where she had this morning, right next to officer Bailey's car. He'd beaten her there by five minutes and was waiting for her with his flashlight at the ready.

"Well, whoever was here has been long gone." He greeted her with that statement as she walked over to him. They both stood at the bottom of the hill looking up at the entrance to the woods, with their flashlights pointed that way.

"Well, let's go see shall we?" She headed up in the direction of the crime scene. The techs had already taken everything they needed but there was no harm in coming back here in case they'd missed something.

The place had a different feel to it at night, eerie, lonely. As she looked around the area she saw once again in her mind's eye, the clown nailed to the tree. Her mind kept coming back to that too. The clown and the acid; two very deliberate additions.

There was a picture forming in her head but all of the pieces didn't fit. If Riley O'Rourke had been Sonya Davis' lover, why did he decide to kill her? And if he had, why had he done it in this way?

There were so many other ways, ways that wouldn't have ended up with the victim practically at his backdoor. She'd heard the stories of women being doused with acid in other parts of the world because they'd rejected the advances of some suitor or other.

But this went much further than that; someone had died. And what about the clown? If as her husband said she was afraid of clowns then someone had purposely set out to scare her. She looked from the direction of the tree where the obscene thing had been found and back to the marked area where the puddle and the body had been.

Between these two places was the place where she'd found the wire that she was sure had been placed there to do exactly what it had done. But would a lover go to such lengths? It didn't add up. There was something missing.

She just couldn't see Riley O'Rourke doing the things that had been done here, and the question still remained, why? "I need to get a look at her room at home." She started back down the hill with the light from officer Bailey's flashlight leading the way.

She heard an engine approaching and stopped on her way to the truck. From the way her skin prickled as if from an electrical charge, she knew who it was before he exited the Land Rover.

"Mr. O'Rourke? What are you doing here?"

"I came to see who was up here. Did you find those kids?" He seemed more annoyed than was warranted when he slammed the door and walked over to tower over her.

"We've got it under control..."

"A woman died here, they shouldn't be allowed to just come here and trample this place like that."

"It was just morbid curiosity I'm sure Mr. O'Rourke. We'd already taken what we needed from here, no harm done."

He didn't seem too satisfied with her response and she found herself becoming annoyed. "Where is your wife Mr. O'Rourke? I still need to ask her some questions."

"Not tonight." Why is he so persistent that I not talk to his wife?

Riley turned and headed back to his truck without another word, slamming the vehicle into drive before driving back to the farm. He'd snuck out of the house because he didn't want to disturb his wife who was having a rough time.

The pills he'd given her must've been more powerful

than he thought because she'd been sleeping for hours, which was good all things considered. She'd lost her best friend of almost thirty years and he knew it had hit her hard.

He'd been standing at the back window gazing into the dark at nothing, his mind on Sonya and the day's events when he saw the lights up in the woods and guessed correctly that it had to be kids roaming around out there. He hadn't thought twice about picking up the phone and calling down to the station, but he still had to go see for himself that they'd been run off. Damn kids!

He idled the truck into its parking space and walked up the steps to his quiet house. Usually this time of night the TV would be going, and the soft cadence of conversation could be heard, but not tonight, tonight everything was deathly still.

He was as quiet as possible when he opened the back-door to walk in, but it was in vain. She was in the kitchen, tying her robe around her waist, fresh from her bath. She looked up with a frown when he walked in. "Where were you?"

"Uh, I went up to the woods. There were some kids up there earlier messing around the crime scene." He'd wanted to keep that from her as well and from the look on her face he knew he'd been right.

He walked over and wrapped his arms around him. "How are you doing Val?" She wrapped her arms around him, resting her head on his chest. He was surprised when she wrapped her arms around his neck and pulled his head down to hers. "I need you."

He opened his mouth under hers, still not sure but letting her take the lead. She seemed hungrier somehow, more passionate than she'd been for quite some time. Not since her last pregnancy disappointment when the stick did not change color.

He remembered hearing somewhere that sometimes people need to reaffirm the fact that they were alive when someone close to them had died. So he went with it when she pressed herself against him, letting him know that she did indeed want him.

He lifted her in his arms and started to head out of the kitchen to take her back to their bed. "No, take me here. I don't want you to be careful with me. I want you to take me the way you used to when we first got married."

His cock came to life at her words and he laid her back across the marble topped island. He tugged the short silk robe open and pushed it off her shoulders to find her naked beneath. "I see you came prepared." He grinned down at her, not showing any of the unease he felt at this turn of events.

He was tentatively waiting for the dam to break. For the reality of what had happened to her friend to sink in. He was sure that that's why she was acting this way, so wild and abandoned. Two things she hadn't been in a very long time. He figured this was just her way of reassuring herself, and who was he to tell her no?

He lowered his head and licked her flesh, feeling that fire in his gut for his woman for the first time in way too long. Things between them had cooled about a year or two ago and he knew it was because of their childless state.

Her inability to get pregnant had driven a wedge between them that no amount of reassurance on his part had been able to fix. He felt like a bastard for thinking it, but he was glad for the change. It had been a long time since he'd felt this level of lust for the woman he'd married and planned to spend the rest of his life with.

Now he put it all out of his mind as he set about turning her body to liquid fire. Her pussy had always fascinated him, with its fat lips that filled his head with visions of running his tongue between them.

He spread her open with his fingers and inhaled her fresh scent before giving her his tongue, diving in deep until she hissed with pleasure. She gripped his hair in her passionate haze, pulling him into her as she moved against his ravishing mouth.

He felt himself harden further and released his cock, taking his heated flesh in his hand and stroking as a string of precum escaped its tip. "Now Riley, I want you now." He left off eating her out and stood to his full height of six foot two.

Looking down between her thighs he led his cock into her until he was fully seated, his cock swelling to its fullest inside her as he closed his eyes with remembered pleasure. He'd always liked being inside her, and didn't expect that to change, though lately...Better not go there Riley, not now.

He brought his complete focus back to her and ran his hand down her middle to where they were joined, flicking her clit with his thumb as he surged into her. "Yes!" She hissed out the one word as her hands came up to cup her breasts and squeeze.

His eyes followed their movement and he grew even harder inside her, wondering at this new fire in her, a fire that he'd not seen in a very long time. Not that he was going to complain, he liked her like this, had missed this side of her in fact.

Because though her appetites had waned, his were still in full force. He loves to fuck and made no bones about it, and when she'd withdrawn from him and the marriage it had been hell...Once again he dragged himself back from those wayward thoughts and turned his full attention on her once more.

It wasn't long before her wild actions, the way she tugged on her nipples and gyrated her hips as he fucked into her had him close to cumming and he leaned over and sucked one of her nipples between his teeth.

A nipple she held up for him. He bit her none too gently because he knew how much she liked that and it wasn't long before he felt the quivering deep inside her, drawing his seed from him.

FOR THE REST of that whole night she kept him busy. After he was done with her in the kitchen he took her off to bed because that's what she wanted. Her body finally gave out after she'd ridden his cock for the second time and fell against his chest too tired to move.

He held her close and kissed her head before rolling her off of him and onto her side of the bed. He watched her sleeping face in the moonlight that came through the window and wondered at what was going on in her head. He hoped that he was able to chase away the demons at least for tonight. He'd deal with tomorrow when it got here.

He took a quick shower to clean up and his stomach growled as he flicked the water off. He rubbed it and dried off, before stepping out of the shower and heading down to the kitchen in search of something to eat.

He remembered why he'd missed dinner when he saw it sitting on the table under the cover Eileen had placed over it hours ago and his eyes went to the kitchen window in the direction of the dark woods before looking back at the food that should've been eaten hours ago.

It would be cold now for sure and he wasn't in the mood for the heavy meal of steak and potatoes this late at night. He looked at his watch, or this early in the morning rather. Valerie had certainly been in some kinda mood tonight. He smiled as he opened the fridge for fixings for a sandwich.

CHAPTER 8

etective Sparks hit the ground running the next day. Throughout the night she'd had many thoughts running through her head, thoughts that had kept her awake long into the night; things she'd overlooked the day before.

Her first call as she was walking out the door was to Mr. Niall Davis.

"Good morning Mr. Davis, I know it's a bit early but I have a question for you. You wouldn't happen to know your wife's passcode to her phone would you?"

"Of course, it's zero six nineteen, we both used it; it was our anniversary, why?"

"We're trying to establish her movements yesterday. Someone texted her before she left the house according to your nanny."

"I can't imagine who; Sonya didn't know anyone except me, and the O'Rourkes."

"Thank you sir. Will you be in your office later in case I have any more questions?"

"I'm not going in today, the children...I'll be at home." They hung up and she pocketed the phone as she climbed into the police issue car.

Her next stop was the art gallery where she sat outside waiting for Valerie O'Rourke. Officer Bailey was heading into the station to check up on the leads from the day before per their agreement the night before. She checked her watch for the third time hating the feeling that she was twiddling her thumbs, but it was still too early to call her guy in tech.

Valerie O'Rourke woke up feeling sore in all the right places. She rolled over in bed her hand stretched out to the place where her husband was supposed to be and found it cool to the touch.

She frowned as she sat up, her eyes falling on the bedside clock. It was still early, too early even for him. With a foreman, an overseer and an abundance of farmhands on the job he has no need to be anywhere this early in the morning but he did like to keep his hand in.

She got up and headed for the shower to wash the stink of stale sex from her body. Last night was the first time in a long while that they'd gone at each other like that, and the pleasure she felt from the memory helped to keep her mind off of her friend's death.

She was trying very hard not to think about it, about the way she'd died; how horrible if the rumors were true. She didn't want to imagine the horror she must've felt. "Poor Sonya." She decided as she turned the water off that she'd go into work later, she'd stop by the house and check in on Niall and the kids first. It's what her friend would've wanted.

Because she kept shying away from thoughts of Sonya it was hard to think of what to do next. She knew Niall would be helpless in the face of this sudden tragedy and as their oldest and dearest friend she was perfectly willing to help pick up the slack.

She took her time drying her hair, her eyes following the marks her husband had left on her body the night before and she felt that sweet tingle between her thighs. Maybe they could have a repeat tonight, she thought as she perused her closet for something to wear.

Once dressed for the day she headed downstairs but there was no sign of Riley.

"Where's my husband?" Eileen turned around from the stove at the sound of her mistress' voice. "He left before I came over this morning. Might be something to do with the sick calf I suspect."

"Oh yes, I forgot about that in light of what else has been going on."

"Oh yes, you were so distraught when you came home yesterday I didn't get the chance to tell you how sorry I am."

"Yes, she was a dear friend." Valerie's voice tapered off in sorrow.

Eileen plated the egg white omelet she'd prepared with slices of grilled tomatoes on the side and placed it in front of Valerie before getting her a cup of coffee and some orange juice. "No grain toast this morning?"

"No, you know I only have it once a week."

Valerie closed her eyes in bliss at her first taste of coffee. She caught the housekeeper staring at her when she opened them again and could well imagine what the other woman was thinking.

"I think I'll go see Niall and the children this morning, make sure they're okay." Her face and voice was sullen as she cut into her eggs and she found that it wasn't going to be that easy to put the whole ordeal out of her mind.

She didn't mean to come across as cold and uncaring, but she's never been able to deal with death. She's one of those people who withdrew from such things as a way of protecting herself; a defense mechanism if you will.

She finished her meal for the first time in a long time, suddenly ravenous from the night before and got up to leave for the day. "We'll have roast lamb for dinner Eileen, it's Riley's favorite. And maybe a fresh peach cobbler with some of that homemade ice cream you made and put in the freezer."

She left after giving the woman her orders and hopped into her red convertible. As she pulled down the lane she saw her husband's Rover coming back from the direction of the woods. She felt a slight pang in the pit of her stomach and rubbed it away.

It was obvious that he was taking the death almost as hard as she was, as she knew he would. Was she being selfish? Only concerned with her own needs, she wondered? She hadn't really given much thought to him since Sonya had been more her friend than his, though the two had got to know each other very well over the years.

Still, she should've known that the death would hit him just as hard. She blew her horn and waved when he got closer and he drove over, stopping next to her. "I think I'll go look in on Niall and the children before I go in. What do you have planned?"

"I have some paperwork to take care of then I guess I'll go check in on them as well sometime this afternoon." She nodded her head and put the car in gear. "I'll see you later then." She smiled and started to drive off but he stopped her.

"Hey, I thought you might take the day off, you know, because of..." His voice tapered off because he still wasn't sure how to broach the subject. He'd decided to let her be the one to bring it up when she was ready.

"No-no, I think it's best that I keep busy, that way I won't sit around and think about it. I'm afraid if I stop moving I'll never be able to pick myself up again. It still hasn't quite set in that she's gone you know."

Riley regretted bringing it up at the look of sadness on his wife's face. Yesterday she'd been a mess. He'd never seen his always well-put together wife that close to unraveling before and he knew that the wildness of the night they'd shared was a result.

But he knew that nothing could hold back the grief that she'd face in the coming days and wanted to be there when the enormity of her friend's death finally hit home. Maybe it was a good idea for her to keep busy like she said; everyone has their own way of dealing with loss. So he nodded his head in agreement, putting his own unease aside for now. "Okay, if that's what you want."

"Were you just in the woods?"

"Not really, I just drove up there but I didn't get out. I'm still finding it hard to accept you know. She was so close. While she was being murdered I was not more than a few hundred feet away in one of the barns looking after the sick calf."

He wiped his hand across his face and shook his head as his wife nodded her head and drove off. She was acting just the way he'd come to expect. In the last few years she'd gone from a sweet, bright, fun loving girl, to this cold person he hardly knew.

Last night he'd seen a glimpse of the woman he'd married, but he was afraid there was something else beneath it. Like grief, the grief of losing someone very close to her. He'd just have to keep an eye on her is all, make sure he was there to catch her when she fell as he was sure she would.

She was wound so tight there's no question that she'd hit a wall soon. He headed back to the house to grab some breakfast since he'd missed dinner last night, his mind going to the beautiful woman who'd lost her life and the children she'd left behind.

Sonya had been such an integral part of their lives he was finding it hard to accept her passing, he didn't think he ever would. It was harder when someone as young and vibrant as she was lost their life no matter how it came about. But the way she'd died... He shook his head to dispel the images that intruded.

He was going to miss their chats and truth be told their secret meetings. Meetings that neither his wife nor her husband would've understood. He shook his head once more as he entered the house, leaving the climbing morning heat behind him.

Detective Sparks checked her watch again for the third time in as many minutes. She was late, the gallery was supposed to be open half an hour ago. "What an idiot. Ugh!" She slapped herself on the forehead. "Of course she won't be coming in today, her best friend just died."

She sat and thought of her next move before deciding against going out to the farm. She'd give the grieving friend one more day or a few more hours at the very least. She made a U-turn and headed back in the opposite direction towards the station house. There was plenty for her to do in the meantime.

She'd called the tech with the passcode while waiting in the car for Mrs. O'Rourke to show up but he'd called back with the news that it hadn't worked. That got her mind going again. Why would a married woman change her passcode from the date of her wedding anniversary?

Had there been tension in the marriage? A falling out of some kind? Or was she hiding something? It made sense, the lengths she'd gone to. Why go to all that trouble if she didn't have something to hide?

She pulled into the parking lot outside the ranch style red brick building that housed the police station. There were only five fulltime staffers here, and a handful of volunteers when they were needed.

She'd already been fielding calls from the mayor and knew that if she didn't have something soon to keep him off her back he'd bring in the state patrol. Something she didn't want to happen, because she didn't want to lose her first real case since moving to the small town.

But the way things were looking she didn't hold out much hope that she'd be left at the helm. Time was of the essence but no amount of time was going to help if she didn't get a clue as to what was going on. And going over and over the case in her head was only leaving her with more questions than answers. What a mess!

"Morning boss! I've already got started on those leads like you said but I don't think we're going to find any help there. Two of the places that ordered the acid are commercial cleaners, office buildings, that kinda stuff and the rest are housekeepers."

"I've spoken to a few of them and we can go have a talk with them if you'd like, but they're all sixty if they're a day. I don't see any one of them going into the woods and nailing that freakish clown to a tree and all the rest of it. And I didn't find a connection between the victim and any of those women."

"All the same we'll go talk to all of them. It's the only lead we have now that we're getting nowhere with the phone. Did you hear from Andy?" He shook his head and went back to his computer screen.

Detective Sparks went to her own desk to go over her notes one last time before heading out again. There was something niggling at the back of her mind but she couldn't quite grasp what that something was. Whoever had done this had given it a lot of thought.

At first glance it may seem like an accident, just a string of coincidences that came together to bring forth this one disastrous outcome. But it was too clean, too compact. The clown, the trap, and the acid waiting for the victim to fall into.

If any one of those things were off by just a smidge the whole thing would've been avoided. So how did they know that it would work? How had they calculated so precisely? She was sure that whoever it was hadn't stuck around otherwise old man Doss would've seen them or at least heard them running off.

The key was in there somewhere she was sure. She needed to get into that phone, to at least have that thread to tug on before she could move forward, but the phone was a dead-end unless she found the new code and she was certain Niall Davis would be of no help there.

"Let's go Pete, I want to take a run at those housekeepers but first I think we need to stop by the Davis place on the way. There're some things I forgot to ask him." She headed for the coffee pot in the break room and poured some lukewarm coffee in her carry mug after dumping in enough sugar to put her in a coma and a good dollop of cream.

She didn't miss the look on Pete's face, it's a running argument between the two of them, how bad her sugar intake is, but he let her off easy this time with just a shake of his head. "You know people are already speculating as to what really happened." He mentioned as he held the door open for her.

"Old widow Connors stopped me on my way in this morning to give me her take."

"And what did she have to say?"

"Witchcraft of course and she knows just who's responsible."

"Let me guess, her neighbor Mrs. Ivory."

"You guessed it. They've been at it again; she swears Mrs. Ivory sprayed her hedges with something that's killing it. She wants us to come out and take a look." She nodded her head and made a note of it.

This was a once monthly occurrence, them having to go out there to keep the peace and it wouldn't make a difference to the eighty year old woman or her seventy-eight year old neighbor that they had a murder to solve. Life in a small town sure had its little peccadilloes. But she wouldn't change it for anything. She's never once missed her life back in the city, and was now entrenched in this place she now called home.

CHAPTER 9

*V*alerie rang the doorbell and waited for the housekeeper to open and let her in. It was still early in the morning, just a little after eight, a time when Niall would usually be at work, but she'd guessed correctly that he would take the day off.

"Morning Nettie, how is he?" She smiled at the woman who looked a bit harried this morning.

"About what you'd expect I guess. The children have been a handful this morning and he and Bridgette are trying to get them settled."

The older woman moved over to the side table to wipe a water spot left by the glass Mr. Niall had sat there the night before. It was more for something to do with her hands than anything else. Ever since the day before she's been on pins and needles with worry.

The last time there'd been a murder in this town she'd been little more than a child so it hadn't affected her as much, but this was too close to home. She hadn't been overly fond of the woman she worked for, but still.

To die so young and in such a horrible way if the rumor mill was true, only a heartless person wouldn't feel compassion for the poor soul. Valerie was still thinking about the news about the children, she'd comforted herself with the thought that they were too young to really understand and would not suffer as much.

"Oh no, I thought Junior might be old enough to understand but not Andrea and Abigail. Surely they're too young aren't they?"

"Well, they might not understand death but they know that their mother's not here like she usually is. Poor little mites, they hardly slept a wink according to Bridgette." Nettie sighed and turned to look at the other woman.

"You'll find Mr. Niall upstairs with them!" Nettie turned and headed back towards the kitchen where she'd been busy cleaning up after breakfast and left Valerie to find her way upstairs to the nursery. She'd been here often enough to know her way there.

Valerie felt strange being in the home now that her friend was gone. Her eyes landed on the large portrait of Sonya that sat above the fireplace in the great room as she walked by. She didn't stop to look as her heart raced in her chest and she begun to feel sick. It was finally hitting home that she was gone, that she wasn't going to come bounding out of one of the rooms with that infectious grin on her face.

She made her way up the stairs where she could hear the slight din of voices and came to a stop in the doorway to the nursery. Niall was seated on the floor with little Abigail on his lap, a faraway look on his face.

His eyes were red as if he'd been crying all night and she felt helpless standing there with nothing to offer but empty words and meaningless platitudes. "Good morning Niall, hello children." She walked into the room and he looked up with a ghost of a smile on his face.

He looked nothing like the always well- groomed dashing businessman she was accustomed to and it broke her heart just a little. Yesterday when they came here she'd let Riley do most of the talking because she was still in a state of shock, now she was on her own she found herself still at a loss for words.

He put the baby down and gestured to the nanny, what was her name again? Oh yes, Bridgette. Valerie barely spared the girl a glance as he came towards her in the door. "Let's go have a cup of coffee on the back porch." She nodded her acquiescence and they turned and left the room to the sound of the babysitter trying to entice the kids to play some game.

Out on the porch sitting at the little round table that they'd shared so often in the past, she wished there was something she could do to cheer him up. Some poignant words that would help lessen the burden of grief. He seemed so lost and alone, like he didn't know what to do next. It was a side of him she was accustomed to seeing and wasn't very comfortable with.

Of the four of them Niall was the oldest by quite a number of years. He was forty-three, eleven years older than his wife and her, and eight years older than her own husband. He was always the most stalwart member of their little group.

Not that he didn't know how to have fun, but in the last couple of years, a little after Abigail was born to be exact, he'd become different; more withdrawn, cold, even distant she'd say. That cold reserve he was known for among his peers had turned to ice.

Some days it was almost like dealing with Jekyll and Hyde. Like the time she'd seen him in the next town over looking nothing like himself. It was the way he'd been dressed, even the way he'd walked had seemed different that day.

And when she'd called out to him he'd seemed a bit surprised, almost as if he didn't recognize her. Then suddenly he'd shaken his head and seemed to come out of some fugue state, but had still seemed a bit confused now that she thought of it.

She'd entertained the thought for a moment, just one moment mind you, that he'd been having an affair. Only later she'd found out different. That it was her dear and trusted friend who was getting it on with someone else.

She didn't approve and when Sonya had bragged to her about her new lover and all the things they'd been getting up to she'd told her friend as much. But the other woman had just laughed in her face. She wouldn't say who this new man was, and Valerie had spent countless hours trying to figure it out.

There weren't that many influential men in these parts, no one that fit the type of man her friend would go for and thinking about it had only made her more uncomfortable as time passed.

Now she was here sitting across from this man who was mourning her friend and she had such guilt. There's no way she was going to tell him about that though. But it was like the proverbial elephant in the room.

"How're you holding up Niall?" He took a sip from his cup and stared off into the distance before shrugging his shoulders listlessly. "I'm hanging in there as best I can I guess." She crossed her legs and turned fully around in her chair.

"You've got to hold it together for the kids. I know it must be hard, me myself, I haven't even allowed myself to think about it, so I can only imagine...Anyway, we're here for you, Riley and I."

"How're you two getting along?"

"What, what do you mean?" She barely refrained from snapping out the question as she sat forward.

"Well, I'd noticed just lately that you two seemed to be having some sort of problem. I guess I was too selfish to care very much. Now..."

"Oh we're fine." She waved her hand dismissively as she sat back comfortably in her seat. "He's just been busy with the farm what with calving season just over and now a few sick calves; but we're good." Now it was she who took a sip of the hot brew more to hide behind the cup than for any real need for more coffee.

She hadn't thought anyone else had noticed the strain between Riley and her; she'd gone to great lengths to hide it after all. In a town this small news travels fast and everyone is always in everyone else's business.

She knew the slightest sign of a tear in the fabric of her marriage and tongues would start wagging. She hated that, hated the thought of pitying looks from the town's people, people she'd known all her life. Or worst yet, being the leading topic on everyone's tongue.

It's one of the things she'd worried about when Sonya had first told her about the affair. She hates change and was worried that if found out, it would put a rift not only in her friend's marriage but in the relationship the four of them shared. It was a good relationship, and she never wanted anything to spoil it. But now...

"What did that detective say? Have they found any leads yet?"

"Nothing, she called and asked for Sonya's passcode to her phone. Apparently Bridgette told her that someone texted right before Sonya rushed out of the house."

He shook his head and looked down at the brown liquid in his cup as if not seeing it. "It just doesn't make any sense. Sonya never went into those woods. I can't figure out why. Did you see her, talk to her?"

"No, at that time in the morning I'd have been too busy getting ready to open the gallery. The last time I spoke to her was a few nights ago. I wish I'd spoken to her, wish she'd have called me..." He didn't say anything and they both tapered off, both lost in their own thoughts.

The housekeeper came out the backdoor just then. "Mr. Davis the police are here." He looked up as though not quite comprehending her words and got absently to his feet. "I'll be back Valerie, unless you need to head to the gallery..."

"No, I'll come with you." They walked into the house together to find Detective Sparks and officer Bailey waiting for them in the den where Nettie had left them after offering them both a cup of coffee, which they'd both declined.

"Good morning Mr. Davis, Mrs. O'Rourke, it's good that you're here, I wanted to ask you a few questions as well but you weren't at the gallery when I went by."

"Sit down detective." Niall took a seat and gestured to one of the many stuffed chairs across from him.

"That's okay sir. I just wanted to ask you if you'd let us go through your wife's things." His eyes widened and he shook his head before opening his mouth to speak.

"No, I want her things to stay exactly as she's left them. She wasn't killed here detective I see no reason for you to go rifling through her things. Didn't you already go through her phone? Who was it that texted her?"

"That's just it, the passcode you gave me isn't the right one..."

"What? That can't be, we've used those same numbers for years. It was the day we got married..."

"It's no longer working and the code has been encrypted. We need the code to access any valuable data that might've been left on the phone. Do you know of any reason why your wife would've gone to such lengths sir?"

"I don't know what you mean."

"She's trying to say that poor Sonya had something to hide. How dare you?" Valerie felt herself begin to sweat.

What use would it be for the man to learn now at this horrible time that his wife had been unfaithful? It's bad enough that she had to live with the guilt of carrying that secret; the least she could do now was protect him from that ugly truth.

"Mrs. O'Rourke we're not jumping to any conclusions, we're just trying to understand what's going on. I think if we're given access to her things there might be something there to shed some light on what was going on in her life before this happened."

"No way, now get out. How dare you come here and imply..." Niall jumped to his feet enraged, feeling like he was going to be sick. All night he'd tossed and turned, trying to make sense of this whole situation. Not knowing what she'd been doing out there in those woods...

Detective Sparks put away her trusty little notebook and offered an apology. She knew before coming here that this wouldn't an easy request and had half expected this very outcome.

"I'm sorry that I've upset you Mr. Davis, but this investigation has just started and already we're running into dead ends. My only interest is in finding the person who did this to your wife. I'll leave you to think about it. Give me a call if you change your mind."

"I'll walk you out." Valerie offered as she got to her feet. She walked over and bent down to give Niall a goodbye kiss on the cheek. "I guess I'll head to the gallery now, I'll call you later. Detective!" She turned and gestured towards the door before following them out.

"You said you wanted to talk to me detective, do you mind following me back to the gallery? I don't want to do this standing around out here." She looked around at the neighboring houses with a look of disdain on her face.

"No need for the neighbors to be sticking their noses in." She walked down the stone steps ahead of them and entered her car, driving away without waiting for a response.

"Well, looks like we're back to square one." Detective Sparks looked back at the door they'd just left before turning and walking down the steps herself. "I thought for sure he'd be more cooperative. What did you make of that?"

They both got in, she in the driver's seat as he buckled up. "Of what, you mean him saying he didn't want his wife's things disturbed? I guess I can understand that."

"Yes, but if it helps the investigation..."

"Boss, we're the ones who have to figure that out, for him, he's just lost his wife, his life is never going to be the same again."

"But shouldn't he want to know?"

"Of course he does, but right now I don't imagine that's the most important thing on his mind. Just give him a coupla days..."

"We don't have that long. The mayor's already making noises about calling in the state police. He doesn't seem to think we're equipped to handle our first murder case." And that was still grating on her nerves.

She'd been first in her class at the academy and had gone on to make a name for herself at the precinct where she worked before her life got turned upside down.

Her captain had praised her to high heaven when he recommended her for the job here, and though she'd done little more than rescue kittens and break up fights down at the pub between locals and idiot visitors since making the move, she hadn't lost her touch.

"Well, let's just find another way around it then shall we." She looked at her partner, always so laid back. He still had that college boy shine to him all these years later. She hadn't been that innocent since she was twelve.

CHAPTER 10

Valerie reached the gallery just ahead of the cops and opened the doors, turning on the lights and getting the coffee started at the little station she kept in back.

She'd had an assistant once, but found that the girl spent more time on her phone than she did working, and since her place was never overly busy except when she was having a showing there was no longer a need.

Sonya had always helped out when she needed a hand in the past before the children came, but that hadn't been for a while. As she thought of her friend she wondered how long it was going to take until she no longer did. It was going to take some time she was sure, they'd been such good friends.

They'd done practically everything together, except have children. That was the only place they'd differed. They'd gone away to college together, been married close together;

there was so much that they'd shared in their lives. So many milestones.

She didn't want to dwell too much on it, not now, and especially not with the cops at her door. They came in just as the first drop of coffee dripped into the carafe. "So, detective, you wanted to ask me a few questions?" She didn't see anything wrong with letting them see her displeasure. She was in mourning after all.

"Yes Mrs. O'Rourke, I came by the ranch yesterday but your husband said he'd given you something to help you sleep. I never got the chance to say, but I'm sorry for you loss. I understand you and the victim had been very close."

"Yes, we were, we grew up together, here, in this town. Well Sonya lived outside of town but we went to school together here." Valerie walked over to the huge picture window that lined the front of her gallery and looked out onto the street where she could see people going about their daily lives.

"Can you tell us anything that might help? Who were her other friends? Where did she like to go? Why would she go into the woods? Anything you think might be of help." She turned to face the detective again.

She'd never had any real dealings with the woman before, had never heard her mentioned really since she'd moved to town years ago and took the job. But now that they were this close she was surprised to find the other woman as beautiful as she was.

She had an exotic look to her. Midnight black hair with curls that spiraled down her back and over her shoulders. Wide bright blue eyes that sparkled in the sunlight coming through the glass.

But it was her mouth, perfect cupid bow lips with just a touch of gloss and those high cheekbones that women were going under the knife these days to achieve. She'd have expected to see someone like that on the runway or in one of her paintings hanging on the wall.

"I'm sorry what?" She shook her head and walked away from the window. Detective Sparks didn't think much of the way the other woman had been staring at her, she got that a lot from people who were seeing her for the first time.

It was a curse and a blessing all in one her looks. It was because of her looks in a roundabout way that she'd had to move here. The idiot who'd become fixated on her after one ill-fated date had decided that if he couldn't, as he'd put it, 'possess her beauty' then he'd destroy it.

There wasn't much she could do about her face bar fore-going makeup which she did while she was working, so she usually paid it no mind as she did now. "I asked if you knew of any reason why Mrs. Davis would've been in the woods."

The woman got a very telling look on her face, one that she tried to hide by lowering her head before she walked away, headed for the coffee station that was partially hidden behind a half wall.

"No, I can't say that I do." There was something in her voice and both Celia and officer Bailey looked at each other askance. "It would really help us if you could tell us what you know; anything."

Valerie came back into the room with the steaming cup in her hand, her eyes still trained on the floor. "Well, I don't really know how to say this but, Celia did tell me something more than a year ago."

"And what was that?"

"It's a secret, I'm not very comfortable sharing..." Valerie looked at the two of them undecidedly, making their suspicions rise.

"Ma'am, your friend is dead. If you know something that

may shed some light on the situation you will only be helping her."

"Well!" She pushed her hair behind her ear and walked further into the room. "She said she was having an affair." The words burned her tongue to say and it was obvious to the other two that they made her very uncomfortable.

"Who with?"

"She didn't say and I didn't push. I didn't say anything because doing so would serve no purpose at this point. Unless... unless it was her lover who killed her. You don't think..." She approached Detective Sparks with a horrified look on her face.

"Tell us everything she told you about this lover." Now we're getting somewhere, Celia thought. I knew we were headed in this direction all along; it was the only thing that made sense. Her face gave nothing of her inner thoughts away though as she reached for her notebook.

"Well, not much to be honest. She was very secretive about it like I said. She only shared the fact that she was having an affair. If I remember correctly it was right after I'd commented on the noticeable change in her. You see, after Abigail was born, Sonya suffered from horrible post partum depression."

"She and Niall both seemed to be very stressed, which was understandable with the children coming so close together. I tried to help out as much as I could but," here she waved her hand to encompass the room, "things were very busy around here at the time."

"Maybe if I'd been more of a friend this wouldn't have happened. If I'd paid more attention...Oh hell!" She walked over to one of the chairs and sat down, coffee seemingly forgotten.

"You can't blame yourself for what's happened. I'm sure

you were a very good friend." Detective Sparks felt sorry for the woman who seemed to be really taking it hard. No wonder her husband had sedated her the night before; she was actually shaking with grief.

Just then the bell rung over the door and Riley O'Rourke walked in. Valerie jumped up from her seat and rushed to him after placing her coffee cup down on the side table. "Oh Riley it's just so awful." He wrapped his arms around his wife, while looking over her head at the two cops.

"Can't this wait? You can see she's distraught." His voice sounded angry, defensive; and Celia was secretly beating herself up for not being prepared to see him this morning. She wished she knew why he had such an effect on her, especially with what she was thinking.

Why wouldn't Sonya tell her best friend the name of the man she was having an affair with? From all that she'd learned so far the two women had been close for most of their lives, so why tell her about the affair but not who it was with? Unless...

"We'll leave you two alone and as always, if you think of anything else, please give us a call." She held out one of her cards to pass to the woman but it was Riley who reached his hand out to take it. The last thing she heard as they were walking out the door was him comforting his wife.

NIALL SAT ALONE DOWNSTAIRS for a while after the cops and Valerie left. He was trying to make sense of the detective's words that had left him with even more questions now than before. Why had Sonya changed her code? What was she trying to hide?

He tried to recall if there had been any changes in her

behavior the last few months but nothing came to mind It's true that after baby Abigail was born they'd both sorta spun out of control a little bit.

His psychiatrist had put it down to him having a midlife crisis and it was obvious that she'd been suffering the after effects of the birth. But things had smoothed out a lot here lately, and he refused to believe that his loving wife of almost seven years had been doing anything behind his back that would warrant the need for such secrecy.

"No, they must be wrong." He left his seat and took the stairs two at a time and headed for the room they'd shared as man and wife. The nightgown she'd worn the night before she was killed still laid across the chair where she'd thrown it haphazardly, her panties still on the floor where she'd dropped them after taking them off.

He'd forbidden Nettie to come in here to clean up, to touch anything. He wanted the room to stay just as it was, the way she'd left it for the last time, with just the hint of her perfume in the air still.

He looked around the room now, at all the little bits and pieces that reminded him of his wife, still not quite believing that this was all he would ever have left of her. That she would never walk through the door; never lay on that bed in his arms again. The pain was almost too much to bear and he reached out his hand to lean against the wall.

How could things change so drastically from one day to the next? And yet, life still went on all around him he wondered. How was he still breathing when the woman he loved more than his own life would never breathe again? He felt a scream building inside his chest but held it back with force. He had to remember their children, had to hold onto his sanity for their sakes at least.

He walked into the room and sat on the bed with his

head in his hands as his mind ran through their life together. He remembered the first day they met. How he'd been struck by her beauty and her laughter. It was her laugh that had caught his attention that first time.

He remembered that day like it was yesterday. He'd been in a room full of people, bored out of his mind with yet another get together for the rich and powerful of the state. It was one of those workshop type things where the well established were lending a helping hand to the up and comers.

This venue had been a whole lot different though from the norm, set as it was in a more festive milieu. More like a party where the two groups were meant to get to know each other, than the usual stuffy businesslike settings where those things were normally conducted.

She'd been standing in a group of people with Valerie by her side. He knew Valerie since her dad had been a mentor of sorts when he was younger, but he'd never met the vivacious woman who stood beside her.

When he walked over under the pretense of saying hi to Valerie, introductions had been made and from that moment on she was his. Neither of them cared too much about the fact that he was older than she by eleven years give or take. The age difference was lost in the shadows of the love that blossomed between them from the start.

It was just magical, love at first sight if you believe in such things. His first wife had divorced him years earlier because she said he was never home. They'd been married young, both from good families right here in the little town where he'd grown up and returned after college.

He'd been heart broken then, but it was only after meeting and marrying Sonya that he realized what true love really was. The love he'd had for Anna was more friendship than romance or passion, and he'd counted himself lucky that the amazing young woman had come into his life when she did.

Sure they'd had their ups and downs over the years, especially after Abigail was born. But life had been getting back to normal and they'd been well on the way to getting things back to the way they used to be. And now this, a most unexpected turn that he wasn't sure he'd ever get over.

He felt a deep aching pain, like a blazing ball of fire in the place where his heart was supposed to be. He wanted to rage at the unfairness of it all. Wanted to punch a hole in the wall, tear someone from limb to limb, anything to vent the anger that burned in his chest.

But he had to keep it together for the children, couldn't leave his poor babies alone in the world, or he'd be tempted to join their mother. If he didn't have them he didn't know what he'd do. He was barely hanging on by a thread, barely able to cope with the nightmare that his life had become.

His mind went back to the cops and their suspicions. They didn't have to come right out and say it he knew what they were thinking, those bastards. I'll sue if they leak a word of it, he thought as anger overcame the pain for a brief moment in time, giving him the respite he needed.

He was pretty sure that the town's people would have a lot to say as well, just like they had when the two of them had gotten married. There were some who still blamed him for the divorce, and though it had been more than a decade and way before he'd even met Sonya, in towns like this, where lives are so intertwined, no one ever forgets and they hardly ever forgive.

The thought of her name being blackened filled him with rage and he jumped up from the bed and stalked across the room. He picked up his phone from the bureau where he'd thrown it the day before after turning it off.

He had a ton of missed calls, mostly from family and friends, no doubt calling with their condolences. He wasn't interested in hearing any of it. He just wanted his wife back. He made one phone call; to someone who could help, the only one he could turn to at a time like this.

"Niall is that you?"

"Yes Mr. Mayor, it's me." Mayor Calvin Bosch had been his friend since they were little snot nosed brats on the school grounds. The two of them had remained close over the years though their lives had gone in different directions.

Calvin went into politics with an eye on the governorship, while he had followed in his father's footsteps to take over the bank that had been started by his great-great-great grandfather when the town was just a thought on a few people's minds and imaginations.

"I'm so sorry to hear about your wife. I tried calling twice already but there was no answer. I figured you needed some time alone so I didn't bother to drive out there."

"It's fine Cal; look I need a favor. I know your officers have a job to do, but they're heading in a direction that I know to be false."

"Which direction is that?" Niall took a deep breath and calmed himself down before answering. "I think they're trying to imply that my wife was unfaithful, that she was having an affair. I don't know why she was where they found her but I'm certain an affair had nothing to do with it."

"I've already spoken to Detective Sparks, she knows if she can't handle the situation to my satisfaction that she's off the case. I'll just have a word with her don't you worry."

"Thanks Cal, I don't mean to come off as another privileged asshole but my children..."

"I understand say no more. I'll take care of it you just take care of yourself. If there's anything you need, anything at all, you have my number."

"I know that, thanks again Cal, say hi to the family."

The two men hung up, one in deep contemplation behind his desk in his plush office, the other standing in the middle of the room he once shared with his wife feeling lost.

CHAPTER 11

Detective Sparks hung up the phone a little harder than was necessary. Officer Bailey looked up from his desk where he was busy going over the evidence they'd collected so far on the case. "The mayor again?"

"It seems Mr. Davis put in a call to his good friend the mayor to get him to ask us to back off." She threw down the pen she'd been twirling around in her fingers. The phone rang on her desk and she picked it up.

"Sparks!"

"Detective!" It was the medical examiner who handled autopsies for the three surrounding towns. "Your victim was three months pregnant." The news made her sit back in her chair with a sick feeling in the pit of her stomach. Two victims and another cog in the wheel!

"Is there any way to tell who the father was?"

"Sure, we can run that test but we'll need the father's DNA to match it to." Her first thought was that if the man didn't want them going through his wife's things he damn sure wasn't about to give them any blood to test.

"I'll see what I can do." After she hung up she thought about all the avenues she had open to her. If push comes to shove she could always get a subpoena to make him cooperate, but she was hoping it didn't come to that.

On the other hand, if the kid wasn't his...

"Our victim was three months pregnant." She informed officer Bailey who whistled low and long because he understood that the case had just taken a turn for the worst.

"Maybe this is a good thing. If we can find the father maybe that will get us closer to the killer." She listened to him go over all the pros and cons of this new development as she turned things over in her own head.

"I guess we need to start looking at the men in town and maybe the next town over as well. There haven't been any strangers around that I know of." He didn't even stop to think that it might be her husband's child, not the way things were looking.

"Yeah!" If she were having an affair with a married man he wouldn't want her having a child. Her mind went straight away to Riley O'Rourke. She couldn't shake the feeling that he was involved, as much as she hated the idea.

Her thoughts were making her crazy and since she had no real way of knowing at this point if her suspicions were true, she couldn't stand just sitting here twiddling her thumbs while a killer walked around freely.

"Let's go see those old ladies who bought the acid shall we. I need to take a step back from this thing, maybe then I'd be able to see more clearly."

"Aren't you going to tell Mr. Davis that his wife was pregnant?"

"I'll get back to him after he's had a chance to cool

down." As much as she wanted answers, she couldn't forget that the man had just lost his wife. Though if she really was pregnant by another man and he'd found out he could be the one responsible.

On the other hand if the kid was his, wouldn't he have mentioned it? What if Sonya didn't know that she was pregnant? Too many variables and not enough to go on.

"We'll give him two hours and then we'll head back over there." Living in the laid back small town had made her soft. In the city she'd have been on him as soon as she hung up the phone, but here, things had to be handled differently.

She was willing to take things at an easier pace but not too much. It was murder after all, and somebody was responsible. But she didn't want to piss off the mayor and end up losing the case, so she had to walk carefully, something she never had to worry about back in New York.

THEY VISITED the women on the list, who'd bought the acid in the last month or so, but since all was accounted for that too turned out to be a dead end. She walked away from the last house no closer to knowing the truth.

The women were more interested in questioning her about the murder than expounding their innocence once she'd established that they weren't the culprits and she'd barely escaped their expert grilling.

"Let's go see the widow Connor since we're out this way anyway and get this latest fiasco over with, then we'll head back to the Davis house." It was a short drive to the widow's home and when they got there they say the two women talking over the shared hedge that ran along between the sides of their houses.

The two women, one eighty the other seventy-eight, had lived beside each other for the better part of fifty years. They've long had an on again off again relationship spanning just as long and the local cops were called out here at least once a month if not more to keep the peace between the two.

It was more of a local joke than anything else, but the two women sure did keep everyone on their toes. If no one came out to see about their latest duel things could very well escalate into something more.

Detective Sparks was well aware since her first couple of dealings with the dueling widows that it was just attention they were after and didn't begrudge them the time it took to calm them down.

"Good morning ladies." Detective Sparks hid her grin at the way the two women primped and preened when they saw officer Bailey coming. At least this morning it looked like the feud had been put on hold as the two of them expounded to one another about his many virtues and attributes.

"Well now, how you doing little Celia with all this murder and stuff?" They never called her by anything but her given name. "It's coming along Mrs. Connors, Mrs. Ivory." She greeted both and stood back out of the way.

She knew that her partner was the star of the show and had teased him more than once that they had these dustups every once in a while just to get him to come out and play referee.

"Well, I can't say as I'm surprised, that girl was always running all over the place."

"What do you mean Mrs. Connors?"

"We saw her, didn't we Lenore? Speeding by in that fancy car of hers."

"When was this?" The conversation had taken a turn she had not expected and she drew her note pad from her pocket where she always kept it. This neighborhood was well out of the way and didn't strike her, as the sort of place the fashionable Mrs. Davis would frequent.

"Oh, must've been the day before she died if memory serves me right. She was heading to that old barn down at the end of Miller road." Mrs. Connors pointed in the direction of the barn as Mrs. Ivory nodded her head in agreement.

Miller road was one of the only deserted streets in the whole town. It was home to a plantation that had long been out of existence. Last she'd heard some developer had bought the place and was planning to put up some kind of strip mall but the city council had vetoed the deal and it had been sitting empty ever since, for a good five years now.

"What was she doing there?"

"How would we know Celia? All I know is Lenore called me over to tell me all about it. Said she'd been driving like a bat outta hell too. And then the funniest thing, but I could swear I saw a man following after her a little while after."

"I told you that was her husband Constance."

"Now what sense would that make? They have that big beautiful old house, why would they need to go to the barn to do what they were doing?"

"And how do you know what they were doing Mrs. Connors?"

"Well she had hay in her hair, how else did it get there if she wasn't...you know?"

"How do you know she had grass in her hair?" The old woman didn't answer, just turned and ran into her house next door.

"I'll be right back Celia." Her voice came back to them in

a shout. She came back a few short minutes later with a pair of the oldest binoculars Detective Sparks had ever seen. "Whenever I see anything out of place around here I use these. Used to belong to my daddy. They're mighty powerful, not like these new fangled plastic contraptions they make nowadays. I can see the mole on Lenore's ass with these at a hundred yards."

"I don't have a mole on my ass you old biddy." Mrs. Ivory huffed with indignation.

"It's just a for instance Lenore, keep your knickers on. These young people; always think they know everything." She rolled her eyes at the woman who was all of two years younger than her.

The two women started bickering until officer Bailey called them back to order. "Now if you saw that it was her, how come you didn't see the man who was following her?"

"His windows were tinted and he was moving too fast like he had somewhere to be in a hurry."

"I still say it was the husband. I've seen the two of them back and forth down there a time or two in the past..."

"How sure are you Mrs. Ivory that it was Niall Davis that you saw going back and forth to the barn with his wife?"

"Well, I never did see his face I just supposed..." Her words tapered off with a bit of a confused look on her face.

"See, I told you, she doesn't know what she's talking about. That Niall Davis has always been a prissy one, no way in hell would he be caught dead rolling around in that old broken down old barn."

Detective Sparks' mind was already working. She knew that both Niall Davis and Riley O'Rourke drove cars with tinted windows, but so did a few others in the town. It was something to look into. "Thank you very much ladies, we'll be off now."

"Did we help any Celia, officer Bailey?" Mrs. Connors called after their retreating backs.

"You certainly have, thanks again, and if you think of anything else please give us a call."

She didn't bother giving them a card since they already had a drawer full from all the times they'd been out here. Both ladies batted their lashes at officer Bailey as he said his goodbyes. As she walked away she could hear them arguing with each other before she'd even cleared the walkway.

"What do you think Pete?" She asked as soon as he got into the car beside her. "I think we're going to check out the old barn." She nodded her head feeling a real sense of excitement for the first time since she stood over what had been left of poor Sonya Davis the day before. No matter what the woman had done she didn't deserve what had been done to her.

She drove out to the broken down old barn in the middle of nowhere, thinking that maybe Mrs. Ivory was right. She couldn't see the esteemed Niall Davis coming to a place like this. Unless he'd come here to catch his wife in the act. The women hadn't seen any other vehicles on the road that day though, and there had been no mention of anyone else being in the car with her.

So that leaves the only other alternative; that Mrs. Ivory had been wrong in her assessment that it had been Niall Davis' car following his wife and it had indeed been whoever she was having an affair with.

"The grass is trampled here, and look at that." She pointed out the places where the overgrown grass had been disturbed as they made their way from the car to the barn's entrance. The old door was barely hanging on by a thread when she pushed against it with her fingers.

The place was dusty, with rotted beams hanging from

the ceiling, missing siding that left gaping holes in the dangerously leaning shell of a building, and a heavy scent of mold.

Certainly not the kind of place you'd expect anyone to come to for an assignation, not when they were so many more pleasurable prospects. "I can't see her in this place. Not for any reason and especially not for what the widows were implying." Officer Bailey offered as he brushed a string of cobweb out of his way.

Detective Sparks was wont to agree with him and said as much, but it didn't take long for them to know that they were on the right track.

It was when they made their way upstairs, after climbing the treacherously dangerous rotted stairs against her better judgment.

As soon as she walked into the loft she smelt it. If the stale scent of sex in the air wasn't a dead giveaway the blanket that someone had left behind on the matted hay would've told the tale.

"What have we here?" She moved over closer to get a better look, her heart picking up speed when she saw the newly discarded cigarette butts strewn across the old hay. "Go back down to the car Pete and bring me the evidence kit."

She felt silly now that she hadn't quite believed the women's account enough to expect to find anything; the place was a treasure trove, not least of all were the obvious semen stains on the blanket that was obviously relatively new.

They collected the butts and the blanket and searched the place for what else it had to give up but there was nothing more of use to be found. Her mind already working overtime and she resolved to go full steam ahead now, no holds barred. No way was the mayor giving her case to some stuff shirt.

She wasn't sure about Mrs. Connors' assumption that it had been Niall Davis following his wife, but somebody had been here with her and hopefully those cigarette butts and the spilled semen held the answers.

Her last thought as she put the car in drive was that she hoped it didn't lead back to Riley O'Rourke as she tried to remember if she'd ever seen him smoking. She'd hate to think that she had a sick attraction to a man who was capable of murder.

CHAPTER 12

*B*ridgette, the Davis' nanny of a few years danced around her room behind closed doors with a secret little smile on her face. After holding out all this time she finally saw her chance. She knew if she played her cards right she could very well become mistress of the house where she'd been nothing more than a servant until now.

She stopped in front of the mirror long enough to admire her youthful beauty. A beauty she was sure could capture the heart of her boss now that his wife was out of the way. She pressed her hands against the sides of her breasts and leaned forward to peer down at her cleavage in the mirror.

She was young and firm, with a supple body that was in much better shape than the other woman's she was sure, since the late Mrs. Davis had given birth to three children. Although the woman had kept herself in shape when she was alive, there's no way her old used up body could hold up next to hers.

She had no real feelings about the death of Sonya Davis one-way or the other. No that's not true, she was glad the woman was finally out of the way since she'd exhausted all her efforts in her bid to get Mr. Davis to notice her. While his wife had been alive she, Bridgette, had been nothing more than a passing thought to him.

But here in the last few days she'd noticed a change in his behavior towards her. She'd played up her care and love for the kids every chance she got when in his presence and it seemed to be working.

She'd correctly deduced that his every thought would be for his children at a time like this and was using that to finagle her way into his heart. She had no qualms about using her charges in this way either. Why should she?

She'd grown up in poverty, watching as others enjoyed the finer things in life. Girls who didn't possess half her beauty or wit, who were always above her because of their family name and wealth. She'd always been relegated to the background, her beauty being a blessing and a curse because of the hate and jealousy she'd garnered since she became a budding young woman.

Once she'd learned what her beauty stood to gain her she'd made up her mind that she wouldn't spend the rest of her life the same way she had at birth. There wasn't much pickings back in her hometown in Ireland so she'd set her sights on distant waters.

Her only purpose in coming here to America was to make her fortune like so many others had done before her. And now, with the untimely death of the mistress of the house, she couldn't ask for a better chance than this.

Niall had been so in love with his wife when she first came here that she'd almost lost hope. But then there was a period of time almost a year and a half ago when things hadn't been so good between them. She'd tried then to make her move, but before she knew it things seemed to shift again.

They'd both been acting strange for the better part of a year now and she'd been inclined to believe Mrs. Davis at least had been having an affair. Niall had gone strange as well, keeping odd hours, leaving the house in a haste and always on his phone when he never used to be when he was at home with his family.

It seemed that as soon as Mr. Niall left the house his wife was never too far behind and vice versa and she once again seen her chances fading away. She'd even given thought to leaving and trying her luck elsewhere, but the family was sponsoring her residency and it would've made for a sticky situation for herself; something she always avoids at all cost.

But now with Mrs. Davis finally out of the way she wasn't about to let this chance pass her by. She had no doubt that after a respectable period of time had gone by the vultures would start to swarm. All those unmarried women from moneyed families, or those widows of old friends and who knows what else would come calling.

She wasn't about to let anyone else take what should be rightfully hers. She'd raised his children after all, these last four years or so, and why shouldn't she have the life she'd always dreamed of? How were any of those women more deserving than she?

She'd stood at the top of the stairs and listened in when the cops were here earlier. She could read between the lines with the best of them and knew from what little she'd overheard that the cops were leaning towards Mrs. Davis having had an affair, which might have lead to her being murdered.

Now that they'd planted the seed all she need do was give him a little push. It's no surprise to her that the slut had been cheating. Anyone with eyes could see what was going on. All the secret goings and comings behind her husband's back. The phone calls at all hours of the day that would send her rushing from the house. And she was sure that she'd smelled sex on the other woman more than once after one of those escapes from the house in the middle of the day.

Yes, all it would take is a few well-placed words at the right time and she'd soon have his grief turned into hate. And since she'd be the one to open his eyes, wouldn't her turn to her in gratitude? Her spirits rose with her thoughts and she giggled at her reflection.

Now there was only one thing standing in her way. She'd not missed the looks Nettie have been giving her in the past and knew the other woman would not approve, so it was up to her to find a way to get rid of her next.

She stood in the mirror fixing her blouse, pulling it farther down off her shoulders so that more of her cleavage showed. Not too much, she didn't want to give herself away too soon. He was still deeply grieving after all. But she knew better than most that grief can lead to many things, good things.

Nettie had already retired to her rooms over the garage and would be out of the way until tomorrow morning and the kids were already in bed. She'd had the foresight to take precautions that would ensure they didn't wake up in the middle of the night like they had the night before by adding a little something to their juice at dinner. That meant it was just her and Niall alone in the house for the rest of the long night.

She took one last look in the mirror, and spritzed herself with some of her favorite perfume before heading out of the room. She had to make the run-in they were about to have seem casual so she didn't rush her steps.

She was halfway down the stairs when she heard the doorbell ring. She hurried back up again in frustration but didn't go far. Standing on the landing just out of sight of anyone she cupped her hand behind her ear to listen. She heard the detective's voice and held her breath so that she could better hear.

DETECTIVE SPARKS HAD GONE BACK to the station with the new evidence which she'd asked to be rushed. She knew it would take at least a couple of weeks to get any DNA results back from the cigarettes and she was hoping the blanket would give them something as well.

In the meantime she wasn't about to sit at her desk twiddling her thumbs though. With the new evidence and the statements from the widows Connors and Ivory she needed to get the ball rolling. "We're going back to Niall Davis."

"He's going to complain to the mayor again."

"Let him!" She was always amazed at how afraid her subordinates and others were at just the mention of the mayor's name. Where she came from people weren't so deferential to their local politicians; at least not on the surface.

The two of them went over the new evidence and their hopes that it would lead them somewhere. They were both tentatively crossing their fingers that this would be the boost they so badly needed to hold on to their case.

The Davis home looked quiet when they pulled up outside and Detective Sparks shored herself up for the confrontation ahead. Even as she rang the doorbell she was going over and over again in her head the words she was going to say.

"You again?" Niall greeted them at the door with a drink in hand, looking no better than he had that morning when they left. "Sorry to bother you Mr. Davis but something has come up and we need to ask you some questions."

He stepped back to let them in, not too pleased by the interruption. He'd been sitting alone in the dark reminiscing about his wife and trying to come to terms with all that had happened. Only one day and night had passed and already it felt like he'd lived a lifetime in this new hell.

Riley had dropped by earlier after leaving the gallery and sat with him for a while. Almost as if he sensed his friend was just hanging on by a thread, he'd said all the right things, reminding him of the children and the fact that they needed him even more now that their mother was gone.

He hadn't pushed, hadn't speculated or asked any uncomfortable questions like most people have done since he turned his phone back on and started accepting calls. He'd just been there as a friend and confidant, someone to lend an ear.

It was times like this he was glad for their friendship. Though there was a slight age difference between the two of them, the younger man was never short of well-intended and much needed advice when it counted.

He remembered well how the other man had been there for him when he was going through his midlife crisis not too long ago. How he'd done his best to keep his friend on the straight and narrow. Even more how he'd been there for his family, helping his wife with the children when he Niall was hardly of any use to them.

Now he turned to face the cops who'd just walked into his house for the second time that day.

"What is it that you want to know? I'm still not letting you go through my wife's belongings, still not letting you disrupt any more of our lives. And while we're on the subject, I don't think I like where your investigation is going..."

He was beginning to get on her nerves. She was no longer sure if he was victim or suspect but if he continued to get in her way she was going to have to put aside any compassion she may feel because of his loss. So she cut him off mid-sentence.

"This is a murder investigation sir, not some TV show that you can turn on and off at will. And you calling the mayor and asking him to make us back off isn't exactly making you look good. We're trying to find the person who did this and your cooperation would be greatly appreciated but we don't need you. I can get a warrant to go through your wife's belongings which is entirely within my rights as the leading investigator on this case and not you or the mayor can stop me."

Her sharp tone brought him up short and he looked at her as if seeing her for the first time. She'd taken the gloves off; he could see it in her eyes. But how could he get her to understand that he wasn't trying to be difficult, that he was just trying to hang onto every little bit of his wife that he could.

He had no doubt that some things would fade with time, like her scent that was still left in the clothes she'd worn for the last time before leaving the house and on the pillow next to his. He couldn't bear to lose those things, that last connection, not now.

"Maybe this was done by a stranger, someone who saw her and..."

"This doesn't feel like a stranger sir. Tell me this, would your wife go into the woods to meet someone she didn't know?"

"Of course not... at least I don't think so." He deflated as if someone had leaked all of the air out of him and dropped down on the nearest chair. Each time he spoke to them it became more real. He was trying to escape the reality of his wife being gone, but each time the phone rang or there was a knock at the door he was once again reminded of the horror that his life had become.

"Someone lured your wife into the woods and killed her. They had it all set up, the clown, the trip wire." She cut herself off there because she hadn't told him yet about the acid and what had been done to his wife's face.

"Now the reason we're here is because of some new information that has come up and we need to ask you some questions."

"And what's that, what's this new information?" She pulled her notebook from her pocket even though she knew what she wanted to ask.

"You were seen leaving the old barn on Miller road a few days ago...."

"What, what're you talking about? What would I be doing out there?"

"That's what we're trying to find out. It's believed you were seen heading there minutes after your wife was seen heading in the same direction."

"I don't know what you're talking about. I haven't been anywhere near that place since I was a kid and my friends and I used to go sneaking around out there." She made some notes and tried to remember that the widow had said the windows on the car had been tinted so he could be telling the truth. But the feeling of going around in circles was beginning to get to her.

"From the description of the vehicle it sounds a lot like yours."

"Well you'd better look again detective because it wasn't me."

"About the passcode to your wife's phone..."

"I've already given you the only one I know. We both have been using it for years. If she changed it, it have to have been in the last couple of weeks or so. And no, I have no idea why she would've done that, but I already know what you think."

"I don't think anything sir, I'm just trying to do my job."

"And I appreciate that, but you have to appreciate the fact that I've just lost my wife, my children no longer have a mother so you'll excuse me if I'm in no rush to help you muddy her name with your asinine assumptions. Now if you'll excuse me, I'll like to get back to my evening."

Bridgette had heard it all and was now wondering as she heard the door close behind the cops if she could use this to her advantage. Would it seem too forward of her if she went down now like she'd planned to, or should she put it off until tomorrow?

She wasn't too pleased that she had to put her plan on hold, in her mind if she didn't move now it might be too late. A man like him wouldn't stay single for long even though he'd loved his wife, not with three children to raise. And she had no doubt that there were any number of women waiting in the wings.

The phone had already been ringing off the hook and she was sure that well meaning friends would soon be throwing women at him to take his wife's place and it was a sure bet that none of them would think of her for the job.

She went back to her room and sat on the bed biting her nails and listening with ears pricked for every sound that came from downstairs. It was hours later that she finally heard him coming up the stairs and from the way he stumbled into the wall outside her door she knew he'd had a little too much to drink.

She walked around her room debating whether or not she should go into his room, just to see if he was okay, if he needed anything, but from the sounds she heard just a few minutes later she knew he had fallen asleep. Her disappointment was palpable; a whole evening wasted.

She spent the next few minutes staring at herself in the mirror, comparing her attributes to the late Mrs. Davis. What did the other woman have that she didn't?

She couldn't readily see anything; in fact, except for a college education which she could not afford through no fault of her own she'd venture to say she had the other woman beat.

She was younger, and in her eyes way more beautiful. Her body was naturally curvy instead of the boyish thinness of the now dead woman. She hefted her breasts which were her best feature and the thing she knew most men saw first when they looked at her.

She was hoping those two globes and the ass she kept in shape with use of the Davis' home gym would get her at least through the door. As she stood there her mind began to work overtime. She'd made backup plans for her backup plans when she first came here.

She knew that one way or the other she was going to get her hooks into one of these rich men around here. She'd researched the area before taking the job and though the town was a little on the small side, their wealthy men per capita was more than enough for her to do her fishing in.

It beat living in a large city. There was less competition, and less work to be done searching out her prey. Since her employer was one of the wealthiest men in the area she'd been exposed to the cream of the crop in her new home.

She'd made up her mind long ago that she was going to reel one of these men in no matter what it takes; she'd just been biding her time until now. Most of them were already married or too old for her liking; not that she wouldn't have settled if it came to that.

Originally she'd had all hopes of it being her employer who'd fall for her, since he would be the closest male to her day in and day out. But once she'd laid eyes on Riley O'Rourke she must admit to feeling something more than predatory. The man fit all her aspects of a perfect mate, rich, handsome, kind. It hadn't been long after their first meeting that she'd started sending out feelers.

He never seemed interested in anything or anyone though, other than Mrs. Davis that is. She'd noticed an unusual closeness between the two of them but was never quite able to catch them at anything more than friendly bypass. That too could've been her road to success, having something as juicy as an affair to hold over their heads, but either they'd been too careful, or she'd been sorely mistaken. Now from the way the cops were talking it seems she'd been right all along.

She wasn't too interested in that right now though, that ship had sailed and sunk long ago. Riley O'Rourke had never even so much as held her hand, or exchanged an encouraging smile. She had enough sense to know where not to tread.

Now with the death of his wife it seemed she had Mr.

JORDAN SILVER

Davis just about where she wanted him, all she had to do was make her move before somebody else got there first.

An idea formed in her head. It wasn't anything new, just one of her backup plans, something she'd learned years ago from reading the tabloids. While her counterparts in school had been reading textbooks in order to get into the better colleges, she'd been learning how to marry a man of means, or at least entrenching herself in his life in such a way that he had no choice but to pay her, take care of her.

"If I can just get myself pregnant, that would be just as good." She knew that a man like Mr. Niall would care for his child. Her eyes went to the calendar she kept on the wall that among other things kept track of her cycle. She was a few days off but nothing ventured, nothing gained.

CHAPTER 13

*N*iall knew he'd had too much to drink but who could blame him? As if dealing with the death of his beloved wife wasn't enough, he now had the doubts that the cops had planted in his head to deal with. No matter how hard he tried, he couldn't remember any red flags, nothing to say that his wife had been having an affair.

Granted, he spent long hours at the bank, but surely he would've noticed something. She was always there when he came home and he couldn't remember a time when he called her that she didn't pick up the phone.

It's true that they'd hit a rough patch almost two years ago, but she'd been dealing with post partum depression while he was going through his own issues with the onset of a midlife crisis. But they'd both weathered the storm with the help of their individual therapists and a marriage counselor. Not to mention the support of their friends.

As his mind went to their closest friends he thought of Riley and the bond that had seemed to form between the other man and his wife during that time. He never thought of it as anything more than friendship before, but... No, no way would he believe that his wife and the man he'd considered his best friend had betrayed him.

Sonya had loved Valerie too much to sleep with her husband surely and he'd never once seen the two of them act in any way untoward with each other. But the cop's words kept playing over and over in his head.

He hated to give credence to her words, but why had Sonya changed her code without telling him? What other secrets had she been keeping from him? He realized then that the real reason he didn't want the police snooping through his wife's things is because he was afraid of what they might find.

What if she had indeed been having an affair, what then? His eyes went around the room they once shared and he looked at all the places she might've hidden her little secrets. He didn't want to, but he found himself getting more and more upset at the thought that he'd not really known his wife after all.

And what was that about him going out to the old Miller barn behind her? Who had said they'd seen him? He knew for a fact that it wasn't him. Had the person mistaken him because they'd seen his wife? What about the vehicle that was seen? He knew of only one other man who had the same car as him. Again his mind went to Riley and he found himself thinking of the younger man in a new light.

In his alcohol fused state the anger built until he was almost blinded by it. "That bitch!" The words came out slurred and disembodied as he fell back against the pillows, too drunk to get up and go through her things the way his mind wanted him to.

"Tomorrow!" I'll go through her things tomorrow before

that bitch of a detective gets her warrant like she'd threatened. If there was anything incriminating he owed it to his children at least to get rid of it, to keep their mother's name without blemish.

But if it were true that she had been having an affair and if that man was indeed Riley O'Rourke, he'd kill him. He fell asleep on that thought, but his mind was still filled with thoughts of his wife and the last time he'd seen her.

IN HER ROOM two doors down Bridgette heard the murmurings coming from his room. At first she thought he was on the phone, but when he cried out she knew he was having one of his nightmares. It's been a while since she'd heard the sound. In the past his wife had been there to soothe him. Her face reddened as she recalled the sounds that usually followed.

She tiptoed to her door and peeped out into the dark hallway that bore just a soft glow from the nightlight that was left burning through the night in case one of the children awakened.

The light was dull and low to the ground so did not offer much in the way of a guiding light but she was able to make out the door two doors down from hers by the swath of moonlight that escaped into the hallway. She made her way there now, her heart beating out of time as she approached the half open door.

A quick look into the darkened room didn't reveal much. Everything was pitch black except for the bright colored sheets on the bed. She could make out the mound made by his body only after her eyes had adjusted to the dark, and from the intermittent mumbles in between snores it was obvious he was asleep.

"Sonya!" He called out to his dead wife before mumbling a few unintelligible words. She drew closer, keeping her eyes peeled to the floor lest she stumble into something and alert him to her presence. As she drew near she was better able to make out his words and she held her breath in shock.

She saw movement under the sheet he'd thrown over himself and then the sheet was gone and she saw what the movement was. He had his hand wrapped around his cock as he called out to the dead woman.

His mumbled words became clear as he moved his hand faster and faster on his cock, his free hand stretched out as if to hold something or someone in place. When she realized what he was doing her pussy got wet and her heart raced with excitement.

Being as careful as she could, her eyes going to his face in the dark with each breath she took, she got closer and closer, lowering her head until her lips were over his tumescent cock. As his hand moved down, she took the chance that she had been waiting for.

Lowering her head even further, she stuck her tongue out and licked the leaking head of his cock. When he didn't respond by coming awake but seemed to stroke his cock even harder, she did it again, and again, until she was sure he was lost in a dream and not about to awaken.

She sucked just the tip of his cock into her mouth and held still when he hissed. When nothing more was forthcoming she sucked more of his growing cock into her mouth until her lips touched his hand. She didn't dare remove his hand as she sucked him off, lest the movement jarred him awake.

"So good!" His words brought her to a quick stop until she was reassured that he was still dead to the world. She forgot herself as she enjoyed the feel of a cock in her mouth for the first time in way too long. Not that she hadn't indulged since moving to the states.

But with her work schedule and the slim pickings in the town, her pleasures were far and few between. She'd dallied a little with both Nigel Thorne and Gary Wesley when either had had her route, but even those encounters had been rushed and less than fulfilling, what with Ms. Nettie always sniffing around and sticking her nose into everything.

But Bridgette was no stranger to pleasuring men and having them pleasure her, and what's more, she was dang good at it. She'd had lots of practice after all, back home in the boring town she'd grown up in.

By the time she was sixteen she was a good little cock-sucker and she'd venture to say, so was every female in the village. Why it's how she'd been able to buy herself all those nice little baubles she liked, and had she not been caught at sixteen she might still be at it.

But after the grocer's wife had caught her with her skirts above her head and her knickers wrapped around her ankles as her portly husband plowed the young girl's belly, her reputation had been tarnished and all the women in the neighborhood had learned to lock up their men whenever she was around.

Her beauty had become somewhat of a curse, until her luck changed and the agency that had opened up in the next town over offered her a way out. It was a new program for those who wanted to come to America, matching them up with suitable families to sponsor them.

She'd lucked out big time and now it appeared that her

luck was about to change even more and for the better. She got caught up in what she was doing. Mr. Niall after all had a very nice cock. It was much bigger than the other two she'd sampled since moving here and the man himself was a step up from the two men who were the town's only mail-men; except for the volunteers who worked there a few hours a week.

As he fucked up into her mouth in his sleep, she grew bold enough to move onto his bed between his spread thighs. He moved his hand away and she was able to get more of his cock down her throat as she shoved her hand between her thighs and stroked her clit.

Her panties were wet and she could smell her scent as she swallowed the precum that flowed from the tip of his cock. Her fingers made their way into her starved pussy and she had visions of climbing onto his cock to scratch the itch that was burning out of control between her thighs.

She had to warn herself not to make any stupid moves. What if he woke up...Right on the heels of that thought she felt his hand fist in her hair and was sure she was caught. She choked on his cock as he pushed her head down until her nose touched his pelvis.

"Sonya!" He called out to his wife again as his hand held her head harder, pushing it down faster and faster onto his cock. He came in her mouth just as her fingers brought her off, and then he said something that made her freeze in horror.

"You're not her!" She felt her heart drop to her toes, as she held still in fear. She scrambled for an excuse ready to plead her case. Some way that she could use this to her advantage and turn it around on him somehow.

Always quick on her feet she came up with a ready excuse, something that he'd readily believe. She'd heard his wild murmurings while he slept and had come to check up on him to make sure that he was okay and also to keep him from waking the children who were fast asleep in their beds.

It was he who had grabbed her mistakenly, he who had taken advantage of her kindness. She was sure she could get away with it drunk as he was. And wouldn't he pay her any amount of money to keep that a secret? To keep her from pressing charges as was her right?

She had all the angles figured out but as she raised her head up beneath his hand she saw that he was still dead to the world, he'd been talking in his sleep. She licked his jizz from the corner of her lips and climbed down off the bed.

She hadn't achieved her goal tonight but she'd come closer than she ever had in the past. She looked back at him when she reached the door with the promise to do it again, only next time she'd be sure to go a little bit further. She'd be ovulating in a few days, that would be the perfect time.

She went to bed feeling a lot lighter than she had in the last couple of days when everything had seemed so up in the air and chaotic. Now that she knew how strongly he slept when he was drunk, she was sure she could use that to her advantage. All was not lost.

CHAPTER 14

*D*etective Starks answered her phone the next day. It was Saturday yes, but she didn't foresee herself having another day off for a long-long time. She planned to work right through the holiday if she had to, and that's why she'd rushed the guys in the lab the day before.

For as small as their precinct was, they had a network at their disposal that could get them results faster than some places in the big city. That's one thing she could say for the mayor, he sure did have his resources.

The D.A's office was a very big help in getting things moving quicker as well. They didn't want news of the first murder in the town in more than fifty years spreading too far and wide. Tourism was very big here after all, with people coming from all over the country not to mention the world, to enjoy their classic settings and historical sights.

If news of an unsolved murder made the rounds on one of the biggest holiday weekends, one that the town relied on for an uptick in revenue, let's just say it wouldn't be good for business. So she wasn't too surprised that it was the lab calling.

"We've got those results for you."

"I'm listening." She got her pad and pen ready to take down the information but stopped halfway with her pen hovering over the paper.

"You've got to be kidding me, are you sure?"

"Yes I'm sure. Both the cigarette butts from male A and the semen we found on the blanket are a perfect match. And the other butts match the DNA of your female victim."

"Okay thank you!" She hung up the phone more confused than ever and her partner took one look at her face and knew better than to question her at this time.

He knew that look, knew that she wouldn't tell him a word until she'd worked things out in her head to her satisfaction. But he had to admit to dying of curiosity. The case was going nowhere even when it seemed like they were making strides.

Andy in tech still had yet to break the passcode on the phone so there was still no way of knowing who it was that had made the call to the victim that morning, Mr. Davis was still refusing to let them search through his wife's belongings and it seemed they were at a standstill.

The town's people were starting to get a bit antsy because as far as they knew from their television series, these things were taken care of in the amount of time it took to broadcast a forty-five minute show. With the bad guys all tucked away nicely behind the bars of a jail cell and the victim already laid to rest.

It didn't help that seventy-five percent of the population were in their sixties or older. People of that age bracket tend to worry more about these things as it reminds them of their own mortality.

Old Barney Doss couldn't remember anything more from that day when they took a second swing at him and the truth was they were stuck. Unless Mr. Davis eased up and cooperated they were going nowhere.

Detective Sparks was going over everything in her head. The news she'd just received made no sense, but she couldn't refute the evidence so all that was left was for her to go back to the drawing board; and she did just that.

She left her seat and went to the murder board that she'd set up. She studied what little bit she had so far and her eyes kept coming back to the clown and the statement Valerie O'Rourke had made about her friend having an affair. Her mind was off on another tangent but she had to look at all the angles.

Just because the DNA showed that he was there didn't mean that he'd been the one to kill her. She decided not to confront him right away, not before she had more to go on. She'd already shown her hand by letting Niall Davis know about the barn; maybe she should've played that one closer to the vest.

"Let's go Pete." She dragged her jacket from behind her chair where it always was while she worked.

"Where are we going?"

"Out to the O'Rourke farm." He fell into step beside her as they headed out the door into the early morning sun.

"WHAT'S GOTTEN INTO YOU?" Riley grinned up at his wife as she rolled over and sat on his morning wood. She closed her eyes and flung her head back as she bit into her lip. He'd had a talk with her doctor who'd assured him that her behavior was typical for someone who had suffered a loss such as she had.

It was to reassure herself that she was still alive the therapist had said. He was still giving her sedatives to help her sleep since it was at night that everything seemed to catch up to her and her mind wouldn't let her rest.

Only last night he'd caught her crying alone in their bathroom as if her heart had been broken. Now here she was, her eyes bright as she looked down at him and rode his cock. "I love having your cock inside me, it makes me feel alive."

She rocked her pussy back and forth on his cock and planted her hands on his chest for better purchase. Riley grabbed her ass and fucked up into her hard the way she seemed to want it these days. It had been a while since he'd seen her like this, so loose and uninhibited, free.

He hated that it had taken the death of dear Sonya, but he was glad to have this side of his wife back. It would keep him from making a mistake he knew. As long as she stayed like this, the way she used to be, and as long as she kept fucking him like this there wouldn't be even a hint of the temptation to look elsewhere.

He pulled her down so he could wrap his lips around her nipple and felt her pussy juice the way he likes as he shoved his massive cock into her over and over again. He'd always been a man of huge appetites when it comes to sex and this was more his speed. Not the self-imposed pussy drought he'd been through in the last few years.

He could fuck ten times a day and still not get enough, and in the beginning she'd been right there with him. In fact one of the reasons their marriage had worked so well was because she was one of the few women he knew who could keep up with him when it came to fucking.

But things had cooled considerably between them when she failed to get pregnant year after year. Now it looked like his wife was ready once more to fulfill his needs and though he mourned the loss of their friend, he couldn't be happier.

"Come for me you bad girl." He knew how much she loved that, how much the girl who had been brought up to be a lady loved letting her hair down in bed. "That's it my little slut, cum on my cock."

She screamed and bucked hard on top of him as he pulled her head down to his. She moaned into his mouth as he kissed her and came hard deep inside her. As always she hoped that this time she'd catch, that a child would grow inside her. She'd long come to believe that that was the only way to hold onto him, to keep him by her side always.

Riley pulled her off his cock and threw her onto her hands and knees in the middle of the bed as soon as she came down and her pussy stopped twitching. She barely had time to look back over her shoulder at him before he was driving his cock into her ass with force.

Her eyes closed with the immense pleasure as she felt him there for the first time in way too long. Not since they'd been trying for a child in fact, which was way too long ago. "Play with your pussy you nasty little girl, make yourself cum while I fuck you in the ass."

His words inflamed her lust just as he knew they would and she did as she was told as he fucked in and out of her ass faster and faster, driving his whole length into her bowels until she felt overstuffed.

She'd forgotten how much she loved this; how he'd taught her to like it and all of the other dirty depraved acts he'd introduced her to throughout their many years of marriage.

"Don't cum in my ass. I want to suck your cock, want to

feel you cum on my tongue." Her words came out choppy and breathless as she was too far-gone now, caught up in the pleasure that coursed through her veins like wildfire.

Riley sped up his thrusts, excited by the idea of putting his cock straight from her ass into her mouth. She's never let him do that to her before, always complaining that it was dirty even by his standards.

He'd long stopped worrying about getting her pregnant so cumming in her mouth was no big deal. He figured if it happened it happened. If not, there were still his godchildren, Niall and Sonya's children. He'd told himself long ago that he'd make do with that if that's all he had open to him in this life, and there was always adoption.

He put those thoughts aside now as his wife's ass tightened around his cock. He pulled out of her ass when he felt too close to cumming and slapped her ass hard.

"Turn around!" He pulled her head around none too gently by her hair and shoved his cock, covered in her ass juice into her mouth until she gagged and tried to pull off.

His hand in her hair held her in place as he fucked into her neck, her eyes bulging as she choked on his fat cock. "I'm not pulling out!" In fact he wrapped his free hand around her throat to cut off her air even more, loving the sensation of her throat working overtime around his cock as she fought to breathe while he throat fucked her.

It was a new game for them; Valerie had never felt anything like it. The fear that she was about to choke to death on his cock only heightened her pleasure and she reveled in it as he forced her head further down on his cock.

Drool and cock spit escaped the corners of her mouth as she made choking sounds and tried to keep up with his powerful thrusts. Riley for his part was close, very close, but didn't want the sweet sensations to end.

It was a lost cause though, trying to hold out. Because her throat worked around his meat as she tried to swallow while fighting for her next breath and that was all he needed to blast a load of cum down her neck.

He fucked it all into her throat before pulling out and pushing her to her back, and sliding his cock into her waiting pussy. "Good morning you!" He smiled down at her. She laughed and wrapped her arms and legs around him, lifting her cum filled mouth to his for a kiss.

CHAPTER 15

*B*y the time the police showed up at their door the O'Rourke's were at their breakfast table digging into the meal Eileen had prepared for them. The house-keeper slash cook was glad to see her mistress enjoying her food with such relish again.

These last few days since the murder the other woman has been off her food, barely picking at her meals. Now it looked like she was coming to terms with what had happened.

Riley wasn't too pleased to see them back at his door. He'd been hearing whispers even here on the farm and had had to dress down a couple of his guys for letting their tongues get away with them.

Somehow the rumor mill had got it into their heads that Sonya had been some kind of loose woman who was having an affair and that that's what had led to her being murdered. He blamed the two people who were now standing on his doorstep asking for entrance.

"I don't know how much more we can tell you detective." He moved out of the way and let them in but leaving no doubt that he wasn't pleased about them being there.

"Just a few follow up questions for you and your wife sir. Is she here?" Detective Sparks and officer Bailey stepped into the house and came to a stop in the living room while Riley headed back to the kitchen to get his wife.

Valerie showed surprise when she saw who it was that had come calling so early on a Saturday morning. "Good morning detective, officer, what can we do for you?" She seemed more welcoming than her husband who brooded as he looked on with his arms folded and a stern look on his face.

"Just a few follow up questions ma'am." Valerie walked over to her husband's side and folded her arm through his. She looked much more alive than she had the last few days and Detective Sparks couldn't help but notice she had that certain glow about her. Like she'd made love in the last twenty-four hours.

None of your business Celia, she scolded herself as she pulled out her notebook and got down to work. "You've said in the past that you and the Davises were very close, in fact you were their closest friends. There was also mention of Mrs. Davis going through some kind of change after the birth of her third child."

"Yes, she suffered with postpartum depression as I said and was having a rough time of it. I stopped by the house a few times a week just to help out, take the pressure off."

"And Mr. Davis, how was he during this time?"

Riley gave the question serious thought as he was reminded of an experience he'd had with Niall a little over a year ago. "Well, I think I told you or maybe I didn't that he'd been going through a midlife crisis at about the same time."

"Look, it was hard on the both of them having the children so close together. If you're thinking he did this you're wrong, all the way wrong." Riley went on to tell them how he'd seen the couple both looking happy together after they'd both come to terms with life and had started seeing a therapist.

He wasn't sure if he should mention the other thing that her question had brought to mind. She seemed set on blaming an innocent man for a crime he didn't commit...but what if what he had to say had some bearing on the situation?

What if his holding back would hinder the investigation in some way? He wanted it over and done with if only to keep the cops from interrupting his life any further than they already had. "There was something else, something I didn't think too much of at the time."

"And what's that?"

"One day I ran into Niall and he didn't look like himself. He was dressed different and he even acted like he didn't know me when I called out to him, but then he shook his head and seemed to come out of a fog."

"I saw the same thing." Valerie added as she looked up at her husband in surprise. "Why didn't you ever tell me about that?" Riley shrugged his shoulders and looked back at the detective.

"I didn't think too much of it after the fact. I just figured he was having one of his off days. By then he'd been doing much better though so I guess I just put it out of my mind."

"So you're both saying you both witnessed Mr. Davis acting out of character and even going so far at least in your case Mr. O'Rourke as to say he didn't recognize you." Riley nodded his head and looked down at his wife who agreed with that assessment as well.

"Is there anything else?"

"Yes, just one more thing before we go. Did either of you know of Mrs. Davis' fear of clowns?"

Valerie's answer was that she didn't know about Sonya's fear of clowns. Riley hearing this gave his wife a strange look which both Detective Sparks and officer Bailey noticed.

"Sure you do Val, remember a few years ago when you suggested hiring one for Junior's birthday party and she asked you if you forgot that she'd told you long ago that she was afraid of them?"

"Oh yes that's right, but that was so long ago now I'd simply forgotten." She laughed it off lightly and hoped that she hadn't made herself appear suspicious in the eyes of the two cops.

She'd seen enough cop shows to know that every little thing could be held against you. But surely they couldn't expect her to remember every little thing her friend said, especially from so long ago and something that wasn't that important besides.

Detective Sparks gave nothing away with her facial expression just carried on questioning the pair as she tried to fit the pieces of the puzzle together. "Okay, thank you both, that will be all for now."

"I'll walk you out!" Valerie offered as they prepared to leave.

"Tell me," she said as soon as they were out of earshot of her husband, "are you any closer to finding a suspect?"

"We're getting there, Mrs. O'Rourke, we're getting there."

"Good, that's good. I'm sure poor Niall would appreciate it. By the way, thanks for not bringing up what I told you in front of my husband. Sonya was my very best friend. I wouldn't want my husband thinking badly of her even though she's no longer with us."

Detective Sparks nodded and repeated her goodbyes before heading down the steps to the waiting car. She hadn't learned much more than she already knew, but things were starting to take shape in her mind.

"Where to now boss?" Officer Bailey asked, as he got strapped in in the passenger seat. Detective Sparks tapped her fingers on the steering wheel and looked straight ahead before putting the key in the ignition.

"We've got to get Mr. Davis to let us go through his wife's things. I'd like to do it without having to go through the hassle of getting a warrant but if push comes to shove I'll do it."

"How do plan on getting him to do it?"

"I'm not sure but I have to give it one last try." She put the car in gear and drove down the lane away from the farmhouse.

NETTIE LOOKED on as the nanny who she didn't have much use for fed the baby in her highchair. There was something different about the girl this morning but she couldn't quite put her finger on what that something was.

She wouldn't be surprised if the new style in dress and the lipstick had something to do with catching Mr. Niall's eye. If the mistress were still around she wouldn't have dared. These young people today have the morals of an alley cat.

Here it is just three days since the woman died, her body wasn't even cold in the grave yet and this one was already playing up to her husband. Not that Mrs. Davis was deserving of her pity. She'd been another one.

Nettie had suspected that there was something fishy

going on with the woman before she died, but she'd never had any proof and wasn't one for gossip. But now with everyone else already saying it, she was thinking harder and harder about the things she'd overlooked.

She looked over when Mr. Niall entered the kitchen, his bloodshot eyes telling her what kind of night he'd had. Poor thing, to be this broken up over that worthless woman who didn't deserve it.

She hated thinking this way about the woman who was now dead, the mother of those poor babies, but she couldn't deny the truth of what she'd seen with her own eyes.

All the running around, coming and going at all hours of the day when Mr. Niall was hard at work, the very things she'd once excused away were now plain to see, and with everyone else thinking the same thing...

Why even widow Connors had seen her going and coming from the old Miller barn with some man. She didn't believe for a second that the man had been Mr. Niall; the man she knew wouldn't be caught dead in a place like that. And besides, why would he need to go there when he had a house like this to come home to?

If that detective came back here she'd be sure to tell her what she was thinking this time instead of beating around the bush. She knew Mr. Niall was refusing to let them go through her things, but she knew something that might help.

She felt a moment's qualms about going behind his back. She'd been with him for so long, but it was for his own sake wasn't it? The sooner the police got to the bottom of this mess the sooner he could carry on with his life.

She knew he wouldn't be caught up in the murder, she'd already checked with that Nancy Parish the day it happened after the police had come by and she knew that he'd been in his office at the time it had happened.

Nettie could have no idea that the murderer hadn't been on sight when the deed was done, that it had been a setup, a trap laid for the unsuspecting Mrs. Davis. So when the cops showed up not long after she made up her mind to do what she must.

No one had to know that she'd been the one to do it; she'd get their word that they'll keep her name out of it, or else she wouldn't tell them what she knew. But she for one was hoping to get the whole ordeal over and done with, put it behind them.

Niall had awakened feeling a bit under the weather so the last thing he wanted to see before he even said hello to his kids was the cops at his door. "Look officers, I've had a rough night, and I'd like to spend some time with my children. If you want to see me again contact my attorney."

Detective Sparks knew those words meant she had no recourse but to turn around and go back the way she came. It didn't matter what she'd come here to say, once the person invoked their rights, whether they'd been placed under arrest or she just had a few questions, everything had to stop as soon as those words were put into play.

She was surprised though when Ms. Nettie the housekeeper caught up with her at the car door. "Pssst!" The way the older woman kept looking back over her shoulder it was obvious she didn't want to be seen talking to them, so Detective Sparks didn't waste any time getting her to a blind spot beside the house and out of the line of prying eyes.

"Here, I found this when I took some of her things to the cleaners last week. I knew what it was when I saw it because my daddy used to have one just like it when I was a little girl."

"What is it?" Detective Sparks turned the key over in her hand."

"It's a key to a safety deposit box. They haven't changed those things in over fifty years see. If you look real close you'll see the number written on top." Detective Sparks squinted and sure enough there were three numbers etched into the old key that felt like it weighed a ton.

"Thank you very much for this MS. Nettie."

"It's not for you it's for him. I figure the sooner you get to the bottom of this, the better, then he and those kids can go on with their lives." She huffed and looked around as if expecting to see someone.

"We live in a small town; I know I don't have to tell you how much damage gossip can do to a body. Whatever she's done she's gone now, but Mr. Niall and those babies still have to live here. It's best we get this thing behind us before any more tongues get to wagging." And with that Ms. Nettie turned and walked back inside.

CHAPTER 16

"*W*ell that was a complete waste of time." Officer Bailey grumbled when they got back into the car.

"Not necessarily Pete." Detective Sparks put the car in gear and headed back to town.

The bank was only open half a day today and Monday was a holiday. She wasn't taking any chances that something would stand in the way of her getting into that safety deposit box today.

"Well, it's like this; I've already started putting the pieces together in my head and the key Ms. Nettie just gave me just might be the one thing I need to gain access to the answers."

"Are you going to tell me about the DNA?"

"Oh that, I almost forgot. It's hers and his."

"What, but that doesn't make any sense." She nodded her head. "On the cigarette butts and the blanket. Mr. and Mrs. Davis' DNA is the only thing that we found."

"I don't understand!"

"I do, I'll explain it to you later." She called Andy who'd come in today only because he too was now more determined than ever to crack the passcode on Sonya Davis' phone.

"I haven't got it yet but I'm hopeful. I got my hands on a new piece of equipment that's supposed to crack encryptions. I only have it until Tuesday so I'm going to be working on this baby all day. Can't talk now detective." She looked at the dead phone in her hand and shook her head.

"He didn't let me get a word in edgewise." She couldn't be mad at him since she liked what he had to say. As she pulled up to the bank she thought of the legalities of what she was about to do. She was playing it a bit close since she was sure Ms. Nettie wasn't the cosigner of the box, but on the other hand she wasn't breaking in so didn't need a warrant.

The key had been given to her without her even asking so there was no reason why she shouldn't use it. Plus she had the sneaky suspicion that Niall Davis wouldn't mind once she found what she was hoping to.

She walked into the bank and headed to the front desk. "Good morning, I need to get into safety deposit box number nine twenty-three." She showed the woman the key but didn't identify herself as a cop just in case there was an issue.

She'd left officer Bailey in the car for just this reason as well. Since the key had been given to her she saw no reason why she shouldn't use it, and because she was sure her reasoning would hold up in a court of law since she hadn't pressured the housekeeper to give her the key, and didn't even know the woman had one.

The lady behind the desk didn't ask her any questions which is exactly what she wanted as she lead her to the back and into the vault where the boxes were kept. "I'll leave you to it then, once you're done please make sure you lock it."

She turned and left, leaving Detective Sparks to open the box herself with the key she'd been given. Her hand shook with excitement as she put the key in the hole and it turned. Her heart raced when she saw the thin leather volume that she was sure before she held it in her gloved hand was a journal. "Yes!"

She closed up the safety deposit box and put the journal in an evidence bag before removing the gloves she'd put on after the other lady had left. She walked out of the bank and into the car with no real expression on her face.

"Find anything?"

"Yes, I think this case is about to take a turn for the better." She lifted the journal in its protective bag from beneath her jacket and put the key in the ignition. She was almost tempted to let him drive them back to the station so she could dive right in, but there was no point in cracking the case if she were dead; the boy can't drive.

NIALL DIDN'T SEE his housekeeper go outside after the cops and he wasn't interested. Last night he'd had an epiphany and this morning had awakened with a new outlook on life. He was more inclined now than he had been two days ago to believe that his wife had indeed been having an affair.

Though he hadn't been back to town since leaving the bank on Thursday, he was well aware of what the whole town was saying. He'd seen it in the mailman's eyes yesterday morning, had sensed something when Riley came over to see him.

He was still struggling with the idea that it was his

friend, the man who'd lent him a shoulder to lean on that she'd been having the affair with, but stranger things have happened. He was now imagining that the other man had used his weaknesses, everything that he'd shared with him, to get his wife into his bed.

He sat at his kitchen table across from his children, mad at the world and wanting his pound of flesh. To be betrayed by one of them was bad enough, but a betrayal by two people he'd trusted was more than he could bear. Had they been laughing at him?

His mind went to the last dinner they'd shared together as couples and as he thought of that night something tickled the edges of his mind. Something that was as elusive as a lot of things has been lately; something that no matter how hard he tried he couldn't bring into focus.

The nanny smiled at him; what was her name again? Bridgette! Yes, not a bad looking girl. He found it odd that he'd never really noticed her before. But then again, with Sonya around, he'd never noticed anyone else.

She'd been his world his everything and he'd always thought that he and the children were hers. Now he smiled back at the nanny. Why not? If Sonya had been out there fucking around what's to stop him doing it now that she was gone?

Bridgette wondered if he'd woken up this morning and realized that last night hadn't been a dream after all and that's why he was smiling at her now. She felt herself relax at the thought. When she woke up this morning she'd been afraid that she'd gone too far and was worried about the consequences if he did come to his senses and realized that it was she who'd been in his bed the night before.

Niall had no recollection of the happenings in the night he just woke up thinking he'd had a very intense dream about his wife, something that was natural given the circumstances he was sure. She'd been very good at pleasing him in bed, but how many others...

He cut his thoughts off there the pain too raw, too new. As Nettie placed a plate of ham and eggs in front of him he looked down at the food without seeing it. He couldn't remember the last time he'd eaten.

"Why don't you have a little something to eat sir? You haven't eaten in days and you're already starting to lose weight." Bridgette lifted a forkful of eggs to his lips like she'd have done with one of the children and he found himself opening his mouth to her.

She smiled coquettishly as she slid the fork between his lips and did it again. Nettie stood at the sink with a look of total disgust on her face, slamming the dishtowel down across the lip of the sink before turning to leave the room.

"I'll be upstairs tidying the rooms. Do you want me to change your bed today Mr. Niall?"

"What? Oh yes, sure, whatever you want." Bridgette, who had been holding her breath for his answer released it with a come hither smile. He'd refused to have anything touched and she was sure it was his way of holding on to his dead wife. But now it seemed something had changed.

Maybe it was all the talk of the affair that was on everyone's tongue. She'd even got one of her lovers who work at the post office to hint at such when he came to deliver the mail yesterday. She'd told poor Nigel that she was too afraid to do it herself but that the poor man needed to know the truth.

Since Nigel liked Niall, in fact he'd liked both the Davises, one of the only couples to give him a Christmas bonus every year, he'd seen no harm in it. Sure he felt bad for the poor guy. But men who marry much younger women

JORDAN SILVER

should expect something like this to happen. Granted she didn't need to die over it.

"What do you have planned for the day Bridgette?"

"I was thinking of spending the day in the pool." No she hadn't; it was hell keeping up with all three children in the pool, but she saw an opening and was about to take it.

"I figure it's going to be hot today and since the pool is enclosed and it's nice and cool in there it would be the best place for them, get them out of the house and back to doing normal things. I'll just wait until Ms. Nettie is through with her chores so she can help me keep an eye on them."

"Why wait? I'm here; I'll help you keep an eye on them. Why don't you get them ready and I'll meet you there in five?" Her panties were already getting wet from the look in his eyes as he got up and left the table.

She hurried the children upstairs and got them all ready before leaving them in the nursery with a mountain of toys to distract them and headed into her room to get changed.

She tossed the old one piece she was accustomed to wearing when Sonya was alive to the back of her closet and pulled out the sexy micro mini two piece suit that matched her eyes from its hiding place. She couldn't get into it fast enough.

She pulled a sheer wrap around her and headed back to the children, crossing paths with Nettie on the way. She ignored the sour look the older woman gave her and smiled secretly. You just wait until I become mistress here; you'll be the first to go. She was sure the older woman wouldn't approve of her and Niall's new relationship, but she didn't care one wit, it's not like the old bag could give him what she could.

Niall felt like he had a new lease on life. He was determined not to spend another day, another minute on Sonya;

life goes on. And though he didn't plan on catting around town, giving credence to the ugly whispers that he was now coming to believe were true, there's no reason he couldn't enjoy what was right under his roof and seemingly on offer. He hadn't missed the looks the young girl had been giving him at the breakfast table.

With that thought in mind he headed down to the pool, the enclosed pool, to join the delectable nanny and his kids. And when he remembered some of the things he and his dead wife had gotten up to in there, he hurried his step even more.

CHAPTER 17

*B*ack at her desk Detective Sparks was faced with another dilemma. The journal used a pass code instead of a key and she was sure she was about to face the same dilemma as she had with the phone and was still facing there in fact.

She sat behind her desk turning the thin volume over and over in her hand while officer Bailey did some follow up calls. They were still trying to pin down the distributor of the dummy clown which she'd been surprised to learn was a more common product than she'd thought.

Hundreds of thousands of the things had been bought in the US alone and she was sure it would take them forever to get through them all. Luckily for her, she thought, was the fact that she could just cut the little strip of leather that closed the journal, something she didn't want to do unless it was absolutely necessary.

"Let's see here!" She tried the numbers Niall Davis had given her before, their wedding anniversary, and gave a loud yelp of pleasure when the strap fell open. "I'm in!" She answered officer Bailey's questioning look. She settled down to read as his voice droned on in the background.

Riley had left the house hours ago to go make the rounds on the farm. The last sick calf was finally back on her feet and the way his men run things there really wasn't any need for him to be there, but it's something he liked to do.

Today he was using it as an excuse. He'd needed to get away from the house to clear his head. He'd been so focused on Val and her emotions that he'd neglected his. Sonya is someone that had become very near and dear to him. Not just because she'd been his wife's friend, but because of the woman she'd been.

She'd been warm, loving, kind; all the things his wife hadn't been in quite some time. As a matter of fact now that he thought about it, Val had changed for the worst right around the time of little Abigail's birth as well. Poor little mite, she'd brought about so many changes in so many people, none of them good.

He seemed to be the only one not negatively affected by the child's birth. Maybe that's why he'd gone out of his way to be there for the child in her first months of life and even now years later.

Her mother had wanted nothing to do with her because of her illness, her father had been going through his own personal hell and had seemed to blame the child in a roundabout way. Even Valerie had been a bit standoffish with the little girl from the moment she'd been born.

There'd been a strain between Sonya and Valerie there for a while too he remembered, and his wife had even accused him of fucking their friend in a jealous rage. She'd got it into her head that his many visits to the Davis' house while Niall was away was because he had an interest in Sonya and was there to fuck her.

It had taken a lot of talking and yelling to bring her down from that one and talk her out of confronting her friend. Thank heaven they'd weathered that storm without too much damage.

But now he was afraid the rumors floating around town would send his wife back into depression again. Not to mention what she'd said to him that had sent him out to walk the land while he thought things over. She'd confessed to him that Sonya had told her about a secret affair.

Something he vehemently refused to believe, which had enraged his wife for some reason. He recalled the look in her eyes when she accused him. "Are you calling me a liar?"

"No, I'm not, I'm just asking if you're sure you're not getting local gossip and a conversation with your friend mixed up."

"You think I don't know the difference between some-thing she told me and what the local yahoos are saying? She told me more than a year ago, gloated about it really." It was the way she said those words, added to the look in her eyes that made him believe that she was once again accusing him of having an affair with the now dead woman.

But if what she'd said was true that would mean he didn't know Sonya at all. From all their talks he would've sworn that she was a woman still very much in love with her husband. He'd been the one to suggest marriage counseling to them and no one was happier than he when he saw them on the mend.

But if Sonya was having an affair, who was she having an affair with? He ran through the list of men in their small town and couldn't come up with a single soul that would fit the bill. Of course it could be anyone.

Someone she met while shopping in the next town over, someone she met on the Internet or a friend of Niall's anyone. But he was having a hard time reconciling with the fact of any such thing happening.

His wife wasn't inclined to listen to reason and he didn't want to alienate her further, not when they were only now getting back to the way things used to be. So he'd come out here for some fresh air and to clear his head. If this was true, then Niall was going to need him now more than ever.

NIALL HAD SPENT A VERY relaxing afternoon in the pool with his children. His son, at almost seven was the only one of the three who understood what death meant. Even though it was his first brush with death, except for the one goldfish he'd lost when he was four, his little boy was a lot more worldly than he'd been at that age.

He'd enjoyed the lighthearted flirting between him and the nanny as well. Though he felt guilt in the beginning he'd easily squashed that emotion when he remembered that the woman he was being loyal to even in death had betrayed him.

When he thought of her in another man's arms while he'd rebuffed every woman that had thrown herself at him and his money since meeting her, he felt murderous. So why shouldn't he take what the delectable nanny was so obviously offering?

For that reason he'd offered to help get the kids cleaned up and put down for their afternoon nap after the lunch Nettie had prepared for them. He sat on the closed toilet and watched his older daughter at her bath since she thought she was a big girl now and didn't need anyone to wash her, while Bridgette used the other bathroom down the hall to bathe the baby.

By the time he got Andrea dressed she'd put just a pair of pull-ups on Abigail who was half asleep by then. Because he knew what he was about to do, he headed downstairs to the kitchen and gave Nettie the rest of the afternoon off.

"But what about your dinner?" She had a pretty good idea what he was up to. She'd caught a peek at him and the floozy in the pool making eyes at each other, touching when there was no need to. It's true she wasn't very fond of the mistress before she died, especially in the last year or so when she turned strange, but the nanny wasn't any better as far as she was concerned.

She'd thought Sonya too young, too wild for the young man she'd helped raise, and the nanny was even younger and more wild than the other woman had ever been. She didn't know what it was with men that they let their privates lead them.

"I'll order something in, you've been working too hard these last few days. In fact why don't you go see your friends? You haven't done that in a while."

He went to the drawer where he kept extra money for essentials and peeled off three twenty-dollar bills to give her. "It's on me. Treat your friend to a movie or a meal at the diner."

She took the money none too pleased to be thrown out of her home. He'd never done anything like this before, not even when she'd shown her displeasure the first time he brought Sonya home.

Then he'd just laughed and told her the other woman would grow on her. Now he was willing to throw her away for the Irish bitch who wasn't fit to breathe the same air. She should've put her foot down when they first forced her out to bring the younger girl in.

But it had been the mistress's idea and back then he would've done anything to please her. And so she, the one who'd practically raised him from birth, had been shoved aside like unwanted baggage. Now this! She wasn't going to stand for it.

Niall had no idea of the thoughts going through his old nanny's head as she walked away without another word. He was too full of excitement as he turned and hurried back up the stairs to find the nanny.

She was in her room wrapped in a towel putting something on her face as she stood in the mirror. No words were spoken as he walked up behind her and put his hands on her shoulders. If she rebuffed him now he'd walk away, he wasn't a complete idiot after all.

But Bridgette had no intentions on turning him away. Not when he was falling so easily into her hands. "If you don't want this tell me now." They looked into each other's eyes in the mirror. Her answer was to let the towel drop beneath her perky breasts and turn her head so that her lips met his.

The kiss was dirty, as dirty as he'd ever had, with their tongues tangling around each other as their lips met. He wrapped his arms around her from behind as they fed on each other's mouths and it was she who turned in his arms, wrapping hers around his neck. He pulled her in closer until she could feel the need of his heavy cock pressed between her thighs.

His hand came up between her thighs and felt her pussy, cupping her wet heat as she moaned into his mouth. He dragged her over to her bed never releasing her lips as he took her down and came down on top of her.

She spread her legs open wide when he left her lips and made his way down her body. "Oh..." It had been way too long since she'd felt a man's mouth on her there. He drove his tongue into her cunt and she was close, so close.

Niall ate her sweet young pussy like it was the last meal of a dying man. Her juices had their own unique taste, different from his wife... no I'm not going to think about that traitorous bitch, he thought as he lifted the nanny's ass in his hands and brought her closer to his mouth.

CHAPTER 18

*B*ridgette bit into the back of her hand to hide her screams until she remembered that she didn't need to. She'd eavesdropped on his conversation with the housekeeper from the top of the stairs. That's how she'd known to run into the bathroom and push one of the special dissolving flavored tablets in her pussy before he came back to her.

Now he was eating her pussy just the way she knew he would once he got a taste. She knew for a fact that her pussy with its little enhancement was damn near irresistible to men and the way he growled and moaned as he ate her out told her that she'd struck gold once again.

She gripped his hair in her pleasure as she pushed her pussy harder against his mouth. When she came it was hard and long, and she was sure it was the idea of who he was mixed with the pleasure of his tongue that made the orgasm as enjoyable as it was.

When he climbed up her body she was ready for him. Niall straddled her chest with his long cock bobbing before her face. She lifted her head and took just the tip inside her warm mouth, teasing him with her tongue. Niall grabbed her head and pulled it onto his cock, being rougher with her than he'd ever been with anyone before.

Women didn't like calm and gentle, they wanted to be fucked and fucked hard. Otherwise why would his wife, the woman he'd treated like his queen have gone looking for some other man to fuck her?

Bridgette choked on his cock and looked up at him, wondering at the change in him; he seemed almost angry. Niall realized what he was doing, that he was taking his anger at his dead wife out on the girl who was only trying to give him pleasure.

He reached down and caressed her cheek with his thumb as he fucked into her mouth slower, more gently, until his cock stood hard and firm. "Spread your legs, I'm going to fuck you hard."

Bridgette's heart was almost full to bursting. She was on the cusp of achieving everything her heart desired. To be married to a wealthy man, a man who would make all her dreams come true.

As he fucked his cock into her, her head was full all visions of all the things he was going to do for her. All the things she'd seen him do for his dead wife and more. Furs, expensive jewelry, handbags like the ones she'd drooled over in magazines and of course the other woman's belongings and whatever she had in her closet that she might like.

Niall fucked into the succulent flesh of the young girl, marveling at how wet she was. There was a time Sonya used to get that wet for him. His thoughts made him fuck into the body beneath him harder and harder until she cried out.

He felt her pussy clench around him and covered her mouth with his to taste her pleasure as she came around his cock. In the back of his mind as he got close a warning bell sounded and he pulled out at the last minute.

Niall grabbed her by her hair and pulled her up to kneel in front of him, leading his cock to her mouth. Bridgette felt her pleasure wane as she realized what he was doing. Niall came in her mouth with a low groan, emptying his balls on her tongue until they were dry.

He dropped down beside her when he was done and pulled her into his arms. He didn't feel the usual afterglow like he used to with Sonya but he figured that with time it would come. She was the first woman he'd been with since his wife had died what, three days ago? So no wonder it felt different and would take some time to get used to.

Bridgette watched his face and listened to the beat of his heart as she laid on his chest. Niall felt her eyes on him and looked down at her with a smile. No doubt she was expecting more from him, but he wasn't in the mood to talk.

He took her hand and led it to his cock which hadn't gone down completely. "Get me hard again, I'm going to take you until the kids wake up from their nap. Would you like to share my bed tonight?" He didn't give her a chance to answer but rolled over on top of her and slipped his cock back inside her sweet cunt.

Detective Sparks went home later that day with a lot on her mind. She was halfway through the journal, which read like the diary of a woman in the throes of a passionate reawakening, and things were beginning to take form now. The call from the lab just before she clocked out for the day only added more closure to the picture that was unfolding in her head.

"The child belonged to male A." Those were the words that she'd heard. That along with Andy's assurance that he was getting close to decoding the phone were icing on the cake. She wasn't sure what Ms. Nettie had expected her to find when she gave her that key, she'd got the feeling that the housekeeper hadn't been too fond of her late mistress, but she was sure the older woman as she said wanted this to be over for Niall and the children's sake.

The book didn't point her in the direction of the killer but that picture was beginning to form as well. The more she read the clearer things became and she knew that if what she was thinking was true it was going to turn over a lot of apple carts in the sleepy little town.

Then she came upon a sentence in the book, made a little less than a year and a half ago. "Oh dear!" Is this it?" She put the book face down on her home desk as let her mind fit the pieces of the puzzle together.

She hadn't been called on to use her skills in a long time, but she hadn't gone rusty while resting on her laurels. A look at her watch told her that it was too late to go back to the Davis's residence and tomorrow was a Sunday followed by a holiday.

She decided she was going to go over there the next day anyway, but she needed all the players to be there. How was she going to do that without alerting all involved? That was the question. She had to handle this very carefully so that she didn't lose the thread of the plot. She needed to corner the guilty as soon as she made the writings in the book known so that there would be no room for escape.

She thought about it long into the night and accepted

that there was no way to get them all together without giving something away. She'd just have to rely on Niall's discretion to help her out there.

She took a hot shower to wash away the day's grime before making herself a sandwich which she wolfed down while reading the final entries in the journal. It looks like she wasn't going to fall flat on her face after all.

She gave herself a little pat on the back as she went off to bed. That night she dreamt of 'him' again. She knew it was pointless in her waking moments but she had no control over her dreams or where they chose to go. And where they always ended up was in Riley O'Rourke's bed.

When she woke in the morning she gave some thought to calling her partner in to handle the Q&A with her, but decided in the end to let him have his weekend off. It wasn't anything she couldn't handle alone anyway. And since she'd had the night to think her mind was much clearer now.

Her phone rang as she rolled out of bed and she was surprised to see Andy's number. "Andy, don't tell me you're still at it."

"I've got it. The last text was from a number that had been interfaced over another."

"I'm sorry what does that mean?"

"It means that someone used a burner phone to contact the victim using a number that was known to the victim."

"I don't understand is that even possible?"

"It's called spoofing, you should look it up." "Is that legal?"

"Technically yes, unless it's being used to defraud."

"What about the burner phone?"

"Still working on it, those are harder to trace, as you know."

"Thanks a million Andy, shoot me a text with the number that was used will you?"

"Sure thing detective."

"Oh wait, what was the code?"

"BITCH! Can you believe it? Calling yourself that? The lady must've had some serious issues." Or someone else did.

She hung up the phone on better footing now than before it rang. The phone was ringing when she came out of the shower half an hour later. It was Pete, officer Bailey and he was more excited than she'd heard him in days.

"I've got something you're gonna like."

"Do you, meet me at the Davis house in twenty minutes."

"Wait don't you want to know what I've found?" Talk while I get dressed. It's the holiday tomorrow I don't want anyone making any out of town trips while I waste time."

His information was even more useful and was the proverbial nail in the coffin so to speak. She left the house feeling more sure of herself than she had since this whole thing started. There was only one drawback though, the people who were going to be hurt by her revelations.

"I'm GOING to see Niall and the kids are you coming?" Riley rolled out of bed from beside his well-fucked wife. She'd gotten over her snit the night before over dinner when he'd tried once again to convince her that he hadn't been having an affair with her friend.

Well, the truth is he wasn't sure that she believed him but she seemed to have come to terms with the issue. He could only hope that one day she'd come to see the light and realize that although their marriage had lost its spark, he wasn't the kind of man to cheat.

Whatever she had going on inside her head she'd been a tiger in bed last night and he had the scratches down his back to prove it. Now if he could just get her to give up this stupid notion about him and Sonya having an affair he could maybe rest easy.

"Sure, why not? Maybe we can talk him into going out somewhere. It's not good for the children to stay cooped up like that all summer." He gave her a look which she missed and carried on into the bathroom.

He wasn't sure how ready Niall was going to be to go out and about town so soon after the murder of his wife, but he was reminded that his wife for all that he loved her can be very self centered and just a tad bit unfeeling at times.

BRIDGETTE WAS FEELING MUCH BETTER this morning than she had the afternoon before. She'd got Niall to cum in her during one of their fuck sessions the night before, in his marriage bed no less. He'd already pulled out of her three times that afternoon, but that night she'd clamped her pussy down around him just as she felt him get ready to pull out and he'd had no choice.

Sure she wasn't fertile yet, not for a few more days, but now that he'd slipped up once and the earth didn't move she didn't see any reason why she couldn't get him to do it again.

Niall on the other hand woke up with mixed emotions. After the nanny left his bed in the wee hours of the morning because he didn't want his children seeing her leave his room, he'd lain awake staring at the four walls.

The anger he'd felt the day before that had sent him

running into her arms, was fast fading beneath the grief his heart still felt for his wife. Why had he been so quick to believe false accusations against her? There must be another explanation for all the things the cops were saying, for what everyone else seemed to believe.

He looked towards the memory album she kept on her side of the bed. It was this little photo thing that reminded her of upcoming events and as he watched he saw that Riley and Valerie were due here this morning for their usual day before the Fourth brunch. Tomorrow as with every Fourth of July they were supposed to go to the farm for the annual barbecue.

"There will be none of that this year." He mourned deep within in his soul at the thought. For the rest of his life he'd face a lot of firsts without her by his side. Like the first day their girls go off to school, the first time one of the children graduated, got married, had children of their own.

"How could you leave me damn you?" He rolled over and pounded his fist into the pillow next to his, hiding his tears and the great heave of sobs that escaped him as the enormity of the situation hit him in the gut once more.

I want to know, he thought. No matter what it is, I won't stand in the way of the cops doing their job anymore. With his mind made up he left the bed and headed for the shower. He didn't let himself think of what he'd done before or the guilt just might have crippled him.

But he made up his mind that he wouldn't sleep with the girl again. If only to preserve his wife's honor. There were plenty women he could choose for his bed if he so chose in the future. There was no need to take someone his wife had trusted with their children to his bed.

"You picked a fine time to come to your senses Niall,

after the deed is done." Whatever, there was no way to go back now; all he could do is move forward.

He'd made it clear that she didn't have to come to his bed if she didn't want to, that her job wouldn't be forfeit if she rebuffed him. At least he didn't have that on his conscience.

CHAPTER 19

⁓

*D*etective Sparks smiled when she pulled up to the Davis residence and saw the Range Rover parked in the driveway. I love it when a plan comes together, she thought. She'd been beating herself up about how to get the three of them in the same room together and here they were, just waiting.

"Come on Pete, let's go catch us a killer." He was all but jumping out of his skin. His first murder case and it had taken them less then four days to solve it. Well, almost. They still needed a confession, but either way, they were going to arrest someone today of that he was certain.

Niall wasn't as aggressive when he answered the door to the police this time. Given his earlier thoughts he would've been the one calling them after the holiday was over, but it seemed the pesky detective didn't take a day off.

"Detective, officer, won't you come in?" Detective Sparks noticed the change in him when he opened the door and wondered at it. She guessed that was part of the grieving

166

process, and after what she'd read in his wife's journal she had another explanation for what and who he was. She greeted the other couple who got to their feet when she walked in.

"Detective, don't you think you're going a bit too far? It's Sunday for heaven's sake, can't you give the poor man a break from all this?" Riley O'Rourke sure seemed defensive she thought, as if her doing her job was somehow an affront to him.

"It's okay Ri, she's just doing her job I suppose."

"Thank you sir, I'm glad you two are here, this concerns you as well."

"Us? but how? Have you found something?" Valerie sat on the edge of her seat with the Bloody Mary that she'd just been enjoying before the doorbell rang in her hand.

"As a matter of fact." Detective Sparks looked around the room, "where are your children Mr. Davis?"

"They're out back with the nanny, why?"

"And your housekeeper?"

"In the kitchen, why are you asking me these nonsensical questions?"

Niall was beginning to rethink his easy acquiescence. "Just making sure no wandering ears are about that's all. So, as you know we've found some things to go on at the murder scene, things we had not shared with you. It took some doing but we were finally able to get into your wife's phone."

"And?" Niall leaned forward in his chair his Gin and Tonic all but forgotten now. He wanted to hear her next words almost as much as he dreaded to. It's true that he'd made up his mind to be more cooperative but that decision didn't make this any easier.

"Your wife was indeed having an affair with someone in this room, and someone in this room is also responsible for her death but they are not one and the same." She let her words sink in as she took in all their reactions. The tension in the room had gone up astronomically.

"I knew it." Valerie screamed into the silence. All eyes turned to her as she jumped up from her seat and turned a venomous glare on her husband before smacking him hard across the face."

Riley who was too bemused by the news didn't pay his wife's reaction too much mind as officer Bailey dragged her off to the other side of the room away from him with a stern warning to stay put lest he was forced to cuff her.

"I knew you were fucking that slut." Valerie growled at her husband with murder in her eyes. Breasts heaving, ears ringing, she wanted blood, his blood. Oh the humiliation. She'd suspected, oh how she'd suspected, she was nobody's fool. But the lies...

"And that's why you killed her isn't it Mrs. O'Rourke?" Detective Sparks dropped that bombshell and waited for the chips to fall.

"I don't know what you're talking about." Valerie dropped down in the nearest chair and took a great big gulp of the chilling liquid in her glass. She needed the kick of vodka to shore her up some.

"It was a neat trick, buying the acid under your company name. But because you bought the dummy under that name as well, when we cross checked they both came back to you."

"I bought that acid for a new painting experiment, something I'm sure you'd know nothing about, and it's pretty common, besides anyone could've bought it." There was no give in her; no way she was going to let this nobody stick the blame on her for killing that slut.

Niall was still in shock at the news that his wife had

really been having an affair. Suspecting it was one thing but hearing the words spoken out loud like that were shattering. She'd really done it. The woman who smiled in his face every morning, made love to him at night, had betrayed him with another man. How will he ever learn to trust again?

"Wait what do you mean the reason she killed her?" He turned his eyes to the woman in question before looking back at her husband. "So it really was you." He made a rush for Riley but was stopped halfway by officer Bailey.

"Calm down sir, I wouldn't want to have to cuff you, that wouldn't be good for anyone. Now you just sit here and listen." Riley who was finally coming out of his fugue state got his feet ready to charge. "I don't know what any of this is about, but I know for damn sure I never slept with Sonya, she was like a sister to me."

"Some sister!" Valerie screeched as Niall sat back with his head in his hands, rocking back and forth as the truth hit him. Detective Sparks walked over to stand in front of him.

"Mr. Davis, I'm sorry to have given you the wrong impression sir, I had to do it that way for effect. It's a cheap trick I know but it has great staying power. The truth is, your wife didn't have a lover."

"What do you mean? You said..."

"I know, but I might've phrased that the wrong way. I think you should read this." Detective Sparks held out the thin leather bound volume.

"What is it?"

"It's your wife's diary that she kept locked away in a safety deposit box at the bank." Start from about a year and a half ago."

Niall took the offered book and rifled through the pages until he came to the first entry going back almost two years or so. He read the pages and felt like he'd fallen into some kind of vortex, nothing made sense. She was talking about him but it was as if she were speaking of someone else, a stranger.

October first: 'So far Niall's other personality doesn't seem to be dangerous, in fact he seems more interested in having sex than in harming anyone. It's like our honeymoon all over again and I get to have the joy of a lover without the guilt. And the sex, it's so fucking amazing that I selfishly hope the doctor never cures him. Unless he hurts himself or someone else of course.'

He looked up at the Detective, "what's she talking about? What other personality?"

"Keep reading sir, it's all in there." Detective Sparks gave him time to read some more of what his wife had written, watching his face change with each new revelation.

January: 'I've told Valerie about my new lover but so as not to betray Niall I haven't divulged any names. Silly girl I think she sometimes suspects that it's Riley, as if I'd ever betray my best friend for some dick.'

Niall felt his heart contract in his chest as he poured over the words. It was all in there. The way she'd noticed the change in him just about the time she was coming back from her own bout with postpartum depression.

It's the reason she'd insisted he go to counseling and to a therapist. It was she who'd warned the therapist to look for a split personality, she who had diagnosed him before any doctor ever had, because it was she who knew him best.

She'd documented everything and kept it hidden because she was afraid of the two personalities meeting as she put it. She didn't want her husband suspecting her of having an affair, but she wasn't sure how he'd react if he found her journal, how could she explain when the two personalities were so unaware of each other?

She'd borne all of it, running at his beck and call whenever he dragged her off somewhere to some hellhole to have sex. She'd written of the excitement as well as the strain of constantly watching, afraid that one day this other personality would become violent.

He read on until he came to the entry about the baby. April: 'I'm pregnant again, but I dare not tell Niall, who knows what this would do to him. I'm working with his therapist to figure out when would be the best time to tell him. Oh but I want this child.'

"A baby? She was pregnant?" Detective Sparks could only nod her head yes, overcome by the tormented grief in his voice before he turned back to the book.

'I never thought, after all that I'd gone through after Abigail's birth that I could ever want another child, but this child, this child is special. Not that all my babies aren't special, but this child was conceived out of Niall's and my renewed love for one another.'

June: 'I told Valerie about the new baby today, she didn't seem very happy for me, but I guess I can understand that. She and Riley have been trying for so long without success of course she'd feel a way, what with me dropping one every two years like clockwork.'

'She and Riley would make great parents; Riley is excellent with kids. I have to say that in the last year and a half Riley has become like my rock. He's the big brother I never had.'

'He was there for me when I thought I was going out of my mind, before the diagnosis of postpartum depression, and he was there for Niall too when he started going through his midlife crisis not long after.'

'I never told Riley about the split personality, that day he told me that he'd ran into Niall and how different he looked and acted, I was tempted, but I could never betray my man's trust. Maybe some day we can all look back on this and laugh. I hope so. Until then, I'm just going to be there for my husband when he needs me.'

'The doctor said there was nothing we can do anyway, just watch and make sure he doesn't hurt himself when he goes through one of his episodes. But so far the most dangerous thing he's done is take up smoking, usually after sex.'

'Oh, and he fancies himself a lady's man, he even got himself a new cellphone which he uses only to call me. I was a little worried about that one, thinking that this other personality, which he calls Simon was going too far. But the therapist said it was nothing to worry about. As long as he didn't go looking for a new home.'

"It's funny how this thing works. I never did understand the concept of multiple personalities. But apparently Niall's is triggered by stress. I'm just thankful that he turns to me and not someone else. It's good to know that I'm still his ideal.'

CHAPTER 20

*N*iall sat back and closed the book with tears in his eyes. He hadn't been aware that he'd been reading out loud the whole time, and that all the other occupants in the room had heard, plus one more pair of ears that were hidden at the top of the stairs, well out of sight.

"I'm going to be sick." Valerie jumped up from the table and ran down the hallway to the guest bathroom where she was violently ill. Detective Sparks gestured with her head to officer Bailey to keep an eye on her lest she pull a fast one.

"So, I am the one she was sneaking around with."

"Yes sir, we ran some test on the cigarette butts and the blanket we found in the old barn we found on Miller's Road and it all came back to you and your wife. The child was also yours sir."

"Oh no, oh hell, why?" His eyes searched the room as if looking for answers and fell on Valerie who was escorted back into the room by officer Bailey. "You, why did you have to kill my wife? She was a good friend to you, always there when you needed her? How could you?"

He turned his attention back to the detective. "I want to hear it all; what did this bitch do to my wife and child?" Riley at this point had overcome his disbelief and just sat in stunned silence. He knew his wife had been jealous but he'd never suspected, never would've expected her to go this far.

"We finally got your wife's phone unlocked, and the last text did indeed come from your phone, or so it appeared. But what Mrs. O'Rourke did was something called spoofing. In a nutshell what she did was buy a burner phone, that's a phone that's hard to trace and added an app that would allow her to call from one number while making it appear that she was calling from another."

She smiled wanly at his confused look. "It's a bit complicated but we don't need to go into that right this minute. Suffice it to say, we traced the burner phone back to Mrs. O'Rourke, we haven't found the actual phone as yet, but we've tracked down the purchase as well as the purchase for the acid and the dummy."

"You said you wanted to know how it happened. As far as we can tell, sometime in the early morning on Thursday or even as early as late Wednesday night, Mrs. O'Rourke..."

"Don't call her that, her name is Valerie."

"Riley, you..."

"Shut up!" He looked like he could kill her with his bare hands.

"Carry on detective." He flung his hand in Detective Sparks' direction as he sat back in his seat. Outwardly he seemed cool and detached, but inside he was a teeming caldron of hate. He couldn't shake the feeling that this was somehow his fault.

That had he not been as close to poor Sonya as he'd

become none of this would've happened. Or maybe had he paid closer attention to his wife's...Valerie's psychosis he could've seen this coming and head it off. It was obvious that she wasn't all there.

He could've forgiven her anything but this. No way was he going to stand by her like he had in the past; this was the final straw. He felt gutted, wide open and left for dead.

"As I was saying," Detective Sparks continued, "we're not quite sure when but what we do know is that Mrs. ...Valerie used her friend's fear of clowns, used your number, the one you use as Simon, to lure your wife into the woods where she'd laid a trap for her."

"What kind of trap?" This was the hard part. Now she had to tell him that his pregnant wife was missing her face. She cleared her throat and forced herself to look at him. He was going to have to live with that horror for the rest of his life the least she could do was be professional about it.

"There was a dummy dressed up to look like a clown. Your wife's fear made her careless and as she ran away in the opposite direction from which she came, which Valerie was counting on, there was a trip wire in her way."

"She wouldn't have been looking where she was going, scared as she was at the sight of the grotesque clown, so she fell over the wire and landed face first into a puddle of acid that Valerie had left there for just that purpose."

"I didn't mean to kill her you've got to believe me." Valerie tried going to Riley after that statement. A statement she had no idea was being taped by Detective Sparks, but he rebuffed her, holding his hands out in front of him as if to ward her off.

"Don't touch me, you make me sick. What about your godchildren, did you think about them you demented bitch?"

"Please Ri, I didn't mean to kill her, I just wanted to scar her face. Like those honor things you know. I thought you two were having an affair. She'd gloated to me about the affair and when I asked her who with she refused to tell me."

"We've been friends since Pre-K, we never kept anything from each other, so why now? What other conclusion could I draw other than the one I came to? And then she told me about the baby, about a month ago I think it was."

"How could I live with another woman having your child when I couldn't?" There was madness in her eyes now, a madness she'd kept well hidden from the world until now. A madness Sonya had sensed more than once but had over-looked because of her great love for her friend.

"It wasn't mine you pathetic monster. I told you time and time again that I didn't mind that we couldn't have children. Did you think I didn't know that the fault was with you?"

"You...you knew? But how?"

"I had myself tested so there could only be one other explanation. But I didn't care. I even told you as long as we had our godchildren I was fine with us never having our own. How was I to know that you'd see that as me fathering them?"

His voice tapered off at the end and he slumped back in his chair looking defeated. "What a mess; what a bloody fucking mess." He covered his face with his hand, trying in vain to shut the rest of the room out, wishing to be anywhere but here, now.

Niall was still processing everything and not quite understanding any of it. His wife had been having an affair with him behind his back to protect him from his own splin-tered mind. The journal he held in his hand had it all docu-mented and he could just imagine her going through all those hoops to keep their family together, to keep him happy, both as himself and this Simon person.

"Her face; did you say her face was in acid? Does that mean...?" His eyes went to Valerie once more and the look of horror on his face said it all. Valerie stepped back behind officer Bailey at the murderous look Niall sent her way, muttering to herself all the while that it was not her fault, that Sonya should've told her.

"I want her out of my house." Niall was barely holding back his temper. It was only because his children were somewhere about that he held himself in check, otherwise he would've rung her neck, cops or no cops.

Officer Bailey moved to put the cuffs on Valerie but she started squealing and squalling loud enough to send the housekeeper running from the back to see what all was going on.

"You should thank Ms. Nettie for helping us crack the case sir. Without her help we would still be trying to catch our own tails."

"Nettie? What did she do?" Detective Sparks chose to leave the telling of that tale to the woman in question.

"I just did as I was supposed to sir. I've been taking care of you in one way or another since you were no higher than a grasshopper and I figure I'll be doing it 'til the day I die." She turned and left the room leaving no doubt that she too had heard what was being said in the room.

When she reached the bottom of the stairs she sent the nanny such a look that the younger woman recoiled and went back to the nursery where she'd left the children to play on their own. What did all this mean? She wondered, as she saw everything that she'd worked for about to slip out of her grasp.

Back downstairs Niall kept reading his wife's words over

and over as the love she bore him became more evident. How could I ever have doubted her he thought? And to think, last night...in our bed. Now he was the one who felt sick to his stomach. It was sheer strength of will that kept him seated.

Officer Bailey had finally got the cuffs on Valerie and was leading her from the house when she announced her need for the bathroom. Officer Bailey had the good sense to stay rooted outside the door so he could cuff her again once she was done and then led her outside to put her in the back of the squad car.

"I guess I'll be going now sir. I'll be in touch in a couple days or so but you have my number if you need me."

"Thank you detective and please accept my apologies for giving you such a hard time."

"No apology necessary sir, I understood your position."

He nodded his head as she turned her attention to the room's other occupant. She hadn't given herself time to be excited at the fact that he wasn't the murderer; that her judgment hadn't been that far off after all.

The look on his face did not bode well so she kept her goodbye to herself and walked out the door to the waiting car where Mrs. O'Rourke was already making noises about calling her lawyer.

It was the weekend so there was a good bet she would be behind bars for the next couple of days until the courts opened up again. But she was still due her one phone call.

They rode to the station in silence except for the intermittent ramblings of their prisoner who couldn't seem to make up her mind if she were sorry or if her victim deserved what she got. Detective Sparks figured that any lawyer worth his salt would get the woman off with diminished capacity.

The most the other woman would probably face was time in some ritzy hospital for the criminally insane and be out in a few years at most. That wasn't her end of things though so she tried not to let it get to her. Her job was done, or near to it anyway.

She felt more tired now that it was over than she had when she was running around looking for answers. She was both emotionally and physically drained and if she were completely honest she'd admit that part of her angst was for Riley. It was crossing all kinds of boundaries for her to even be thinking of him in these terms, but as long as she kept her true feelings locked away no one would ever be the wiser.

They got the prisoner booked, who was not too pleased and let her displeasure be known to all and sundry. It seems her lawyer was away for the holiday and wouldn't be back until Tuesday.

And wouldn't you know, there were no public defenders on call that weekend seeing as it was a Sunday and nothing ever happened here that would facilitate them working such odd hours.

CHAPTER 21

The two men sat in silence for the better part of ten minutes after they were gone. Nettie, assessing the situation came in with a tray carrying two fresh drinks and left it on the center table for them to have when they were ready.

"I don't know what to say to you Niall, I can't help but feel that this was all my fault. I was only trying to help. I didn't..." He covered his face again and tried to make sense of the destruction of his life.

Niall had been paging through the journal the detective had left with him. She'd made copies of what the D.A might need in the future for which he was grateful, he didn't think he could ever part with the book in this lifetime.

"Sonya wouldn't have blamed you. In fact she speaks very highly of you in here. I didn't even know that she'd been going through so much, and you were there for her; thank you." He was choked up, his heart torn once again as if someone had ripped a fresh band-aid off a sore cut that was just beginning to heal.

"That day you saw me, the say when I didn't seem to recognize you, what was I like?"

"You seemed, happy, like your old self before the whole midlife crisis thing. It was right about the time Sonya started coming back to herself. I should've known something was going on, should've asked more questions. I guess in the end I wasn't as good a friend as I thought."

"What are you talking about? Listen to this, 'today Riley came over to help me with the kids. You should see him with the new baby, it's like love at first sight with those two.'

'She can be crying her head off for hours, and no one can get her to settle down, but as soon as her uncle Riley comes through that door she's cooing and smiling one of her gummy little smiles.'

'I don't know what I would've done without him these last few months. He's been a great help; he freed me up enough to take care of my guy, for which I will be eternally grateful.'

"You see she loved you." And now he knew how much she loved him too. It was all written down in this book, this book that was all he had left of her. He closed the book and held it close to his chest as if he could feel the warmth of her touch through the words that were written there.

They each took their drinks and sipped as they sat in contemplation. Riley didn't even think about Valerie, not because he was cold, but because he didn't have it in him to excuse her behavior. He'd told her time and time again that there was nothing going on between him and Sonya.

He'd done nothing to give her that impression short of trying to help her friend. There was nothing else he could've done to prove his loyalty to her. He'd loved her, supported her, and more often than not stood by her when he shouldn't have. But this was going too far even for a man who'd taken vows.

"I think I should leave you alone, let you get back to the kids. You'll come tomorrow? Sonya wouldn't want you sitting here alone like this." He didn't know what to do with himself. He needed to get away, to think, to get his head together.

He said his goodbyes to the children and left not quite broken, but barely half the man he'd been when he showed up here today. He guessed he should've known that things might end up like this; that it was only a matter of time before Valerie did something they couldn't come back from.

He wasn't worried about his standing in the town where he'd grown up. He knew the place well enough to know that it would all blow over in a matter of months. And since he wasn't directly responsible he was sure he wouldn't get as much hate as his wife. But he wasn't thinking about that.

He was thinking about the friend he'd lost and the horrible way in which she'd died. Jealousy, it was jealousy that had brought this whole thing about. And that cop. He had to give it to her even if he didn't want to.

The way she'd laid it out, had she not found that journal there's a good chance people would've gone on thinking that he was the one having the affair, and worse yet, the one who'd killed poor Sonya. He figured he'd made a narrow escape since it had looked for a while there like she'd been gunning for him.

Instead of going straight home he drove up into the woods where the police tape was still stretched across the area where they'd found the body. Standing there in the early afternoon sun, he couldn't believe that she was really gone.

He tried to remember what he was doing that day. Beating himself up for not being there. He looked from the place where she must've fallen back to his place where he could barely make out the top of the farmhouse where he'd grown up in the distance.

Had she seen it too? Had she thought about the fact that he was so close? That she was that close to someone who could help? What were her last thoughts before she realized it was the end? What a horrible fucking way to die. What was it the detective had said? Her face was gone. Her beautiful face with the bright eyes!

He'd always known that Valerie was envious of her friend's beauty and the way everyone gravitated to her and he guessed he'd been no different. But not once had he been interested in anything more than friendship.

It was the kids that had drawn them together. They'd been friendly before, but after she became ill and he read up on what was going on with her and how best to handle it, he'd made the decision to step up since everyone else was too busy.

Niall had the bank and Valerie had the gallery, plus he'd known how hard it was for her to be around the kids, she was jealous of that too. But why hadn't I done something about it? I knew all this, knew that she wasn't wrapped too tight, hadn't been since her thirtieth birthday.

The problem with her was that she wanted everything to go as planned, but sometimes the best-laid plans can go to shit. He'd made light of her tantrums over the years, had told himself that she'd get over it eventually. He would've rather she'd killed him; then he wouldn't have this horrible guilt that was eating away at his gut.

"I'm sorry Sonya, you didn't deserve that, and you deserved a better friend than me." He walked away from the spot promising himself never to return. As he made his way back to his truck his mind did go to his wife.

Part of him wanted to go to her, to help her. They'd been childhood sweethearts after all; she was the only woman he'd ever loved. But he couldn't bring himself to stand beside her in this. Did that make him as bad a husband as he had been a friend?

He didn't know; what he did know is that he kept disappointing the people around him, the people who depended on him. Now all he had left was the farm and his godchildren. They're the ones who needed him now. He could only hope he didn't fuck up there as well.

Eileen looked up when he walked through the backdoor and from the swollen eyes and red nose he knew she'd already heard. She opened her mouth to speak but he held up a hand to stop her. "Forget it, I don't want to talk about it right now."

"What about lunch?"

"I don't want anything thanks, you go on home." He walked through the house and stood in the middle of the living room looking out the large picture window at nothing. How had his life gone off the rails?

His business was doing better than expected, he had his health and more money in the bank than he could ever spend and right this second none of it meant shit. He felt like nothing would ever be the same again. Like he'd never have another day of happiness.

Turning away from the window, he headed up the stairs to his bedroom. He took one look at the bed where he'd made love to her only this morning, just a few short hours ago and felt sick to his stomach.

He barely restrained himself from throwing up. No way was he going to let her make him that weak. He'd get through this no matter what it takes, it might take some time, but he'd get through it.

He walked over to the bed and stripped it, taking the sheets downstairs and out to the burn pile. Eileen, who had ignored his orders to leave, watched him from the kitchen window with understanding eyes. Things were going to be a little rough around here for the next little while. She'd just have to go into town and have a word with some people.

She'd see to it that everyone knew it was no fault of his, none of it. Hindsight is twenty-twenty and she should've known when the girl started acting strange that something like this would happen.

Should she have told him what she'd noticed? Oh what was the point of all that now? It was too late wasn't it? You could've bowled her over with a feather when Nettie called her with the news. But she couldn't say that she was surprised, she'd long suspected there was something off about Miss. Valerie.

These young people today though, all seem to have mercurial moods. One minute they're fine and the next they can get riled up at the drop of a hat. She didn't think much of the girl's moods, passing them off as just the vagaries of married life.

She'd known all along that they were trying to have a baby. Had seen the disappointment time and again. Especially when the Davises had had their last little girl. She should've known that day when she'd happened to look out the window and seen Miss. Valerie beating her favorite horse bloody that something was afoot; and all the other things that had happened since.

She looked away with fresh tears in her eyes and went to

see about defrosting something for dinner. They'd weathered many a storm together and she was sure they'd get through this one as well, just one foot in front of the other.

CHAPTER 22

After Riley left Niall had stayed sitting in the chair in the living room. The drink in his glass had become watered down and forgotten. His mind was a constant whirl going back and forth with what-ifs. What if he'd done this, what if he'd done that?

He still had no recollection of this other personality, no matter how hard he tried he had no memory of any of the things she'd mentioned in the journal. He read and reread her words so much they became a blur.

He heard the children playing upstairs and his heart broke for them. But at least they didn't seem to be too affected by their mother's absence, thank heaven for small mercies. Only Junior knew that his mother was never coming back and he'd spent some time with his son trying to help him through this trying time for the young boy.

It hadn't quite set in for him either, he hadn't cried for one thing, but he seemed to have this new look in his eyes. Like he'd grown up overnight. He wished the child would cry; get it out of his system. But he knew he couldn't control the child's grief, he could barely get a handle on his own.

It was all so senseless, to think that someone he'd trusted, had let near his wife and kids had done this. When he'd thought that Riley was the one, that had been hard enough, but somehow this seemed even worst; like the worst kind of betrayal.

They'd practically grown up together, Valerie had known Sonya longer than she'd known even Riley. Of the four of them those two had known each other the longest, had been the closest. How had it all gone so wrong?

Bridgette had been tempted to go down the stairs more than once but each time she chickened out and went back to the children. Will this change things? Would he go back to mourning her?

But what about their night together? Can he so easily forget about it, shove her aside? Send her back to being little more than a servant in his home? She felt sick at the thought, how would she face him? Worst yet what if he found someone else?

"No, I have to do something." She rushed out of the room and down the stairs before she lost her nerve. Niall looked up when she came into the room. "What is it? Is it one of the children?" She shook her head and rung her hands, suddenly unsure of herself in the face of his indifference. It's as if he was looking right through her. Nothing at all like the man whose bed she'd shared the night before.

"Listen, about last night." She felt her stomach drop at the tone in his voice, she knew what he was about to say and her mind went in all directions trying to find a lifeline. She couldn't claim pregnancy it was too soon. "I'm sorry, I know it's going to feel like I used you. But last night and yesterday I was mad at my wife."

"You see I was starting to believe the rumors, that she'd been having an affair. Turns out she wasn't. In the end she didn't betray me but you and I, what we did, I'm the one who betrayed her. I'll never be able to forgive myself for taking you to her bed."

He threw up a little bit in his mouth before going on to explain. Bridgette said nothing as he spoke, going round and round in circles with what amounted to a rejection. "What I'm trying to say is, you can't stay here."

He couldn't stand to see her, to look at her, be in the same room with her. He didn't want her in his wife's home, the home he'd shared with Sonya. What had I been thinking? He thought. She could never take Sonya's place, no one ever could.

"I'll give you severance pay of course, and pay for your travel back home if you'd like." She was struck dumb; in that moment she didn't know what to say. All the arguments she'd prepared left her head and she was left standing there with her world imploding around her.

She'd had such hope after their night together and here they were not even twenty-four hours later and he wanted to send her back, back to what? She'd die before she went back there. "What about the children, who's going to take care of them?"

"I'll find someone else, you can't stay here." He felt dirty just looking at her, but he couldn't blame her, it wasn't her fault. At least he's man enough to accept responsibility for his own actions.

He got up from the chair and left the room leaving her standing there and went to his office to write her a check. He gave her three months pay and a little extra to cover a plane ticket home.

Since the holiday was tomorrow and there was no way

for her to cash the check now, he made reservations at the only Inn in town for her to stay for the next few days and paid in advance.

He was sure that would raise some eyebrows in town but he couldn't bring himself to care about that now. He just wanted her gone. He needed to escape the shame of what he'd done.

NETTIE HAD BEEN the one listening in where she wasn't welcomed this time. She'd barely snuck away in time from behind the doorway where she'd been standing listening to what was going on between Mr. Niall and that hussy.

She was glad it hadn't taken him long to come to his senses, that she wouldn't have to suffer the girl for much longer. A lot had changed for her in the last few hours. She felt a certain kind of guilt because of her thoughts about poor Mrs. Davis. To find out that the woman had been doing so much to protect her husband while she'd been suspecting her all the while was a hard blow.

She made up her mind that she was going to make it up to the dead woman by looking after her family, it's the least she could do after all. She went about getting things ready for dinner and didn't even look up when the younger woman came downstairs hours later with her suitcase.

A horn beeped outside, a cab, the only one in town, was here to pick her up. The house felt different as soon as the girl left the house. She couldn't quite put it into words, but there was a new lightness about the place. It felt the same as it did before she came.

Nettie could acknowledge now that she'd suspected the girl of having a hand in what had happened to her mistress, and even though it turned out that that wasn't the case, she was still glad to be rid of her. What would it look like the likes of her being mistress of this home?

That's what she was after, what she'd been after since she came here Nettie was sure of it, so she was only too glad to see her go. Good riddance she thought as she went up the stairs to check on the children. Poor little tykes, two people lost in a matter of days.

No matter, she'd see things set to rights. Just as soon as she got the family over this hurdle and put a stop to the wagging tongues in town, she'd see about hiring some good help. Someone who was more interested in raising the children than jumping into Mr. Niall's bed.

VALERIE WAS GRAVITATING between rage and moments of clarity. One minute she was remorseful and the next she was filled with such hate she'd try to break the bars of the cell in half with her bare hands.

How had she ended up here? She'd planned everything down to the last detail. She'd bought everything under the name of the company, a name that hardly anyone in the town knew or even remembered. It wasn't the same name as the one on the marquee outside the gallery of course, but the name her great grandfather had used for the family business decades ago.

It's an umbrella company that the relatives of her generation still uses, comes in handy for tax cuts and things like that. Along with some other less above board dealings that were better left alone.

She'd never have expected the local detective and that hick she works with to unravel all her hard work so easily.

She thought for sure they'd have written it off as a prank gone wrong, anything but the conclusion they'd drawn; the right one.

And Riley, every time she thought of him the pain was too much. If he'd come here now, just to see her, she could maybe endure this hell. She had no doubt her lawyer could get her out of this, he's been getting her family members out of jams going back thirty years.

And once she beat this thing she wanted her husband by her side. They didn't have to stay here, they could move, escape the gossip, but there's no way she could lose him now. Sonya was dead already anyway so what was the point?

This was partly his fault after all. If he'd listened to her, understood her feelings and stopped running to Sonya and her brats every time they needed him, none of this would've happened.

She paced the cell back and forth, biting her nails down to the quick as her mind worked. She walked back to the bars that caged her in and yelled for someone, anyone. Desk Sergeant Clyde Walker had been looking forward to a quiet Sunday evening before the madness of the holiday the next day.

He was just as excited as everyone else around here that they'd caught the murderer but he selfishly wished they'd done it on his day off. The princess in the cell was treating this place and him like this was the Ritz and he was her personal lackey.

He'd been back there twice already and both times she'd given him an earful when he refused to give her another phone call. He was tempted to do it just to shut her up.

"What is it this time Mrs. O'Rourke?" He couldn't believe he was saying this, never thought he'd see the day. Her husband is easily the richest man in the whole state and a couple others to boot. What reason would a woman like her have to commit murder? And the way she'd done it, just vicious. Looks like the town had been wrong, once again.

Eileen Cline had called his wife just before he left out the house to start his shift and given her the whole story. It was a shame really, all that had happened here in the last few days. Senseless murder over a misunderstanding.

What he didn't get though was why Mr. and Mrs. Davis felt the need to play those kind of games? Granted things around here can get very boring, but two grown people pretending to be strangers, meeting up to have secret trysts with each other was just plain nuts.

To each his own he always says, but at least they got to the bottom of it and a lot of innocent people will be spared the blackening of their names. He stood in front of the cell and waited for her to turn around and answer him.

"I need to call my husband!" The way she was biting into her nails and that wild look in her eyes, he knew if she didn't get her way she'd start that screaming again. It was against protocol, but who was to know?

"How about I call for you?" He didn't wait for her answer but walked across the room to the lone desk on this side of the building where the jail was located in the back of the station house. He asked her for the number and dialed it as she gave it to him.

"Oh hi Eileen, I was wondering if Mr. O'Rourke was available."

"Who wants to know?"

"His wife would like to speak to him..."

"I don't think he wants to do that."

"Look, you'll be doing me a favor. Just ask him to come to the phone."

He heard her rest the phone down on the other end and

held his breath praying for a miracle. He'd heard from his wife who'd heard it from Nettie that Riley had already disowned her. He can't say that he blamed him. Some people may find it cold, but what was the poor man supposed to do?

If she'd subjected him to even a fraction of what she'd been doing here the last few hours he could well imagine the younger man thanking his lucky stars that he was rid of her.

"Clyde, he won't come to the phone, he says he's not interested in anything she has to say." And with that Eileen hung up the phone and went about her business no doubt. He dreaded having to tell this nut that her husband was well and truly done with her.

"What are you doing? Pick up the phone, where's Riley?"

"Im sorry ma'am but he says he doesn't want to talk to you." He took pleasure in saying that to her, she was a real piece of work this one.

She pulled on the bars and started screaming again. "Let me out of here, I have to talk to Riley, I have to make him understand." Clyde walked away leaving her behind and hoping she'd tire herself out soon enough and give him some peace.

CHAPTER 23

~

*H*e turned up his radio to drown out the noise of her screams and rants and pretty soon got caught up in the show that he was fond of listening to, to stave off the boredom that can sometimes set in on those long uneventful nights behind his desk. It was a lot of conspiracy nonsense but he and most of the other men in town got a kick out of it.

It was almost an hour later before he even remembered her and he hoped she'd tired herself out enough to give him some peace and quiet. He bemoaned all those times he'd begged for some excitement around here now that he'd had to put up with her.

He turned the radio down and listened, but all was quiet back there for the first time since he came in for his shift. "Thank heaven." He murmured to himself as if someone might overhear him, though there was no one there.

He started to turn the radio up again when the hairs on the back of his neck stood on end. Had she tired herself out after all? That would be for the best he thought as he made his way back there again.

He knew, as soon as he saw the bottom of her shoes on the floor he knew. His mouth fell open when he came into full view of the cell and saw what she'd done to herself. As an officer of the law who'd been on the job for more than twenty-five years, he'd never seen anything like it. It looked like she'd ran headfirst into the wall.

He ran over to the phone to call Detective Sparks. They couldn't blame him for this surely, no one had said anything about a suicide watch. He couldn't be expected to stand watch over her the whole time she was here now could he?

CELIA HAD BEEN TAKING A MUCH DESERVED scented bubble bath when the phone rang. Thankfully out of habit, she'd taken it into the bathroom with her and answered on the third ring with the glass of chilled wine halfway to her lips.

"We've got trouble, she killed herself.

That was the greeting from the desk sergeant before she could even get the word hello out of her mouth. His words stupefied her for the merest of seconds before she flew into action.

"What do you mean? How did this happen?" She dried herself off with one hand while holding the phone to her ear with the other and ran from the bathroom into the bedroom. She stood next to the bed at a loss, her thoughts splintered into a million little pieces. Clyde was muttering unintelligible words on the other end of the line and she cut him off midstride.

"Call the M.E. and the chief." She hung up the phone and rifled through her closet for a pair of jeans and a tee shirt. Not her usual fare for the workplace but time was of the essence. She called officer Bailey on her way out and he was ready and waiting when she swung by his place to pick him up.

"The chief and M.E. should be there granted no one left the state for the holiday." That was her greeting when he opened the passenger door and climbed in. She was still frazzled by this turn of events, her mind filled with ways she could've prevented this.

At no time had it entered her mind that Valerie O'Rourke would take her own life, she just wasn't the type. After all the noise the other woman had made about her lawyers and what she planned to do to the town once she got out, she thought for sure she'd have her day in court.

Officer Bailey was just as rattled as she was. He'd been catching up on some much needed sleep when the phone rang and his mind had taken a few minutes to adjust. It seems he'd congratulated himself too soon. "What was Clyde doing? Why wasn't he watching her?"

"Okay, we can't start pointing fingers and placing blame, let's just get there and see what happened, then we'll go from there." Her mouth felt dry, and her stomach filled with heavy stones of dread. The one resounding thought in her mind was how she was going to tell Riley O'Rourke that his wife had died on her watch.

"What a mess!" She sped through the narrow streets, which were a lot more lively because of the holiday, ignoring the disapproving looks of the locals as she passed them by. The siren she had blaring meant nothing to them here, not like it would have in the city. Nothing disturbed their slow pace, not even death.

She was pleased and distressed to see both the M.E's vehicle and that of the chief. She hadn't had much dealings with the man since his old friend recommended her for the job, but from what little she knew of him, he was a taciturn no nonsense kind of guy who frowned on excuses.

"Sparks what the hell is going on here? How could you let this happen?" He barked at her as soon as she walked through the door. Sergeant Walker was sitting behind the desk looking white as a sheet with his head in his hands.

"I'm sorry sir, I didn't foresee this development."

"Well you should have. You arrested the wife of the richest man in town for murder and you didn't think this was a possibility? I thought you were smarter than this. What happened to all that fancy training you got in the city?"

She bit her tongue and tried not to play into that particular scheme. It wasn't the first time he or someone higher up had sneered at her background and she knew it was coming from a place of one-upmanship.

She'd gone out of her way in the beginning not to step on any toes because she knew just what they thought of her; but in this case he was right. She'd dropped the ball and the shit had landed square on her foot.

"May I see her sir?"

"Mike's back there with her." It took her a second to realize he was talking about the M.E. Mike Peters before she headed to the back where the cells were located.

Had it not been the weekend and a holiday at that, the prisoner would've been transferred out instead of overnighting here at the county jail, then she would've been someone else's problem. Celia scolded herself for her selfish and less than compassionate thoughts, but she was well and truly sick of Valerie O'Rourke.

The woman had had everything. A husband that most of the women in town under fifty and a few above would've given their eyeteeth to have sitting across the breakfast table from them. A successful business from all appearances, and more money than she could spend in ten lifetimes.

Why did she have to take her life down this path to destruction? What a waste of resources. Celia knew that that wasn't the real problem she had with the woman the M.E. was now examining though. It was the thought of what this would do to Riley that had her so upset.

Even though he'd rebuffed the woman earlier she was sure that he'd have come to his senses eventually and though they may not have reconciled he'd still have some kind of feelings for the woman he loved and had been married to for all those years.

Selfish, that's what she was, selfish and just a tad bit mad. Detective Sparks couldn't really drum up much sympathy for the woman but in her professional capacity she owed it to everyone involved to handle things diplomatically.

"What do we have Dr. Peters?"

"Well, it looks like she took a header into the wall. No defensive wounds, not a scratch on her except for where she bashed her head into that wall over there." He pointed to the far wall and her eyes followed.

Even from here she could see the splash of red against the dirty grey stone of the cell. There was one wound on the deceased's head where she'd connected with the wall, but it was the eyes wide open in death and that look of madness still shining bright that held her attention.

She left Pete to his job and went back to the others. It was hours before the body was bagged and the chief and M.E. got ready to leave the premises. There was a ton of paperwork to be done and she still had to go out to the farm, something the chief had assured her he won't be doing when she asked.

She'd have thought with Riley being the town's leading citizen that he'd have wanted the job. "I'm spending the day with the governor tomorrow, guess what's going to be the topic on everyone's lips then. What a monumental fuck up." He threw the words at her as he moved towards the exit.

She gritted her teeth once more and refrained from reminding him that he'd said the same thing at least twice already. She was in enough shit as it is.

There was no victim services unit, no family liaison, no one to pass the buck to, unless she wanted to burden poor Officer Bailey, which she knew would be a jerk move on her part.

So after the body had been removed and she'd finished typing up her report, she sent him home and prepared to face the music on her own.

"You sure you don't want me to come with you?"

"No, you go on home, at least one of us should get to salvage what's left of this weekend. Oh crap, I brought you here didn't I?" The thought of driving him home and then having to make her way back again was tiring.

"Don't you worry about me, I'll just head on over to the pub, someone will give me a ride home from there not to worry." She walked to the car and got in, suddenly tired to the bone. She'd seen more of Riley O'Rourke in the last few days than she had in the whole time she'd lived here and none of it good.

She tried to brace herself for the upcoming confrontation but nothing could stop the swarm of butterflies in her stomach or the feeling of failure that dogged her heels. Some of her old acquaintances on the force back in the city would call this done and done, but she liked to see things play out in their full course.

She'd much rather have seen Valerie O'Rourke stand trial even if it meant the other woman would've walked away with little more than a slap on the wrist. For her that's when the case was over, it didn't just end with the chase and capture.

She slowed down when she reached the turnoff to the farm still no closer to a decision on how she was going to break the news to him. Will he be angry? Lash out? Her heart raced sickeningly in her chest.

She knew he must hate her; blame her in some round about way for all this. Add the fact that he hadn't been exactly welcoming the other times she came out here, and now that she was bearing even worst news she didn't expect much. "Oh hell!"

This is why she never lets her stupid heart get involved. If it were anyone else she wouldn't be beating herself up like this. She'd have relayed the news, offered her condolences and be gone already. But here she was, sitting outside his home on a Sunday afternoon panicking like she was about to take the state exam all over again.

She realized as she sat there that she was worried not only about how he was going to take the news about his wife's suicide, but how he was going to feel knowing that she'd done it not long after he refused to speak to her.

Sergeant Walker had shared that much with her in an aside. The poor man was feeling guilty and scared shitless that he was going to lose his job and his pension for breaking protocol. She'd promised to keep it just between the two of them and didn't bother warning him against doing it again, she was sure this was a lesson he'd never forget.

CHAPTER 24

*R*iley heard the car pull up outside but didn't bother to get up and look. He'd finally got rid of Eileen and wasn't in the mood to see anyone. He was the only one of his family left in the town; everyone else including his parents having chose to head for livelier climates.

As long as their trust funds were padded they could jet off to parts unknown for months, or sometimes, even years on end. So he really didn't care who was out there and had no plans on answering the door.

He preferred to brood in silence and think about what the hell had happened to his life. There was no one to blame, not that he was into that sort of thing. He's the kind of man who likes to take responsibility for his shit; but life sure had jumped up and bit him in the ass this time.

He picked his head up when there was no knock on the door and no one rang the bell. Not being interested was one thing, but having some jackass sitting out on his driveway was another.

He got up and walked towards the side door where the person had driven around instead of staying close to the front. Baring his teeth when he saw who it was he dragged the door open. She's the last damn person he wanted to see, one, because she'd fucked his life over, and two because she confused the hell out of him.

He'd never had many dealings with her in the past; in fact he'd had no dealings with her whatsoever. They didn't move in the same circles so the one and only time they'd been introduced before this was when she'd first moved to town.

He had no need of her and no uses either, until she'd shown up in his life a few days ago. It wasn't her job, or the fact that she was the one to bring his murdering bitch of a wife down, but something about her, the person.

She didn't look like a cop, not by any stretch of the imagination. Short, but not too short, he'd put her as five-seven to his six-two. Thin framed with her attributes well proportioned or so they seemed beneath the baggy clothes she seemed generally fond of.

It wasn't her body so much that threw him off, it was her hair, her eyes, dammit, it was everything about her. He hadn't had much time to dwell on any of that in the last few days, just enough to note that there was something there.

But since he wasn't the straying type he'd ignored it. It's not like he'd died when he got married. He's surrounded by beautiful women whenever he leaves home on a business trip and was never once tempted.

He wasn't saying that this pain in the ass tempted him either it was just that she didn't fit. He didn't like shit confusing him, didn't like anything messing with his mind unless he wanted it to.

But he was honest enough to accept that the only reason he hadn't paid closer attention to the reasons why she got under his skin was because he'd been too caught up in the murder and what was going on with the people around him.

Now that the shit was solved his mind seemed to think now was as good a time as any to pick that shit apart. "What the hell are you doing here? Haven't you done enough?" She'd finally stepped out of the car and was now standing there looking up at him from the bottom step like she expected him to pounce.

He turned and walked back inside leaving the door open because he knew she wasn't going to leave until she'd said whatever the hell it was she'd come here to say. He needed that drink he'd been denying himself all afternoon after all.

Celia walked through the door and hung back not getting too close. Riley looked over his shoulder at her after pouring himself a heavy shot of scotch. "I'd offer you one but I'm sure you'd tell me you're on the clock or whatever."

"Whatever you've come here for make it quick. The faster you get it over with the sooner you can leave and I can get back to what I'm doing here." Which is nothing but she doesn't need to know that. He couldn't imagine that she was here to do Valerie's bidding after he refused her phone call.

"What is it? Did you come to scold me? Did you think I was being cold earlier when I didn't go after her, take care of her? Did you call me a cold unfeeling bastard in your mind?"

"I'm not cold, far from it. I just happen to believe very strongly in right and wrong and I don't fuck with grey areas. Anyone who gets tangled up in my life has to live by the same creed or I'll cut them loose no matter who it is. She knew that about me, she's always known that."

He was working himself up into a lather and she figured it was best to get it over with before he made himself any angrier than he already was. This couldn't be easy for him no matter what he was saying. It wasn't that easy to cut someone out of your life, she knew that better than anyone.

"Mr. O'Rourke I'm sorry to have to tell you this, but there's been an accident." He stopped with the glass halfway to his lips.

"What sort of accident, what the hell did you do now?" He knew he was being an ass but he wanted her gone.

She was standing there just inside the doorway as if she were afraid to get too close, afraid that he'd do something to her. Fat chance of that happening, she wasn't even his type. He liked blondes, bubbly blondes who had class and style.

Not this introvert who dressed like she bought her clothes at the Salvation Army and he damn sure never dated a brunette before; witch! That's what she reminded him of, with that black as night hair and those light blue eyes that seemed to sparkle in the light.

"It's your wife, she...she killed herself." The words hit him in the gut like a sledgehammer. Of all the things he'd expected her to say that wasn't it. "What are you talking about? Didn't you people watch her? Didn't you know what kind of person she was? What kind of a detective are you?"

He advanced on her and she made herself stand still in the face of his anger. He had every right to be angry and she knew it, but that did not make the situation any less volatile. "Are you happy now? Is this what you wanted?" He sneered at her, the words bitten off between his teeth.

She looked up at him with a crease in her brow not quite

understanding his meaning. "What do you mean? Of course I didn't want her to take he own life."

"You think I didn't notice? Didn't see the way you looked at me, watched me?"

Celia drew in her breath harshly and tried to make herself smaller as he stood close enough that she could smell the liquor he'd drank earlier on his breath. "I don't know what you're talking about." She turned to leave, to make her escape. Later she'll come back later with Pete.

But he grabbed her arm roughly and pulled her back around. It was obvious from the look in his eyes that he blamed her for his wife's death. She tried pulling her arm away, tried to leave once again, her heart broken into a million little pieces. "Where the fuck are you going?" He growled the words before dragging her back into the room and slamming the door shut.

ON THE OTHER side of town the widows Connors and Ivory were sitting on the former's front porch enjoying the nice glass of lemonade heavily dosed with their favorite bourbon.

The sun was just beginning to set and the day was finally cooling down from the hellish heat they'd been battling for the last few days. "Well, I sure am glad that's over."

"You and me both, but I do feel bad for that poor young woman, and here I was thinking the worst of her."

"How were you to know Constance, that she and her husband liked running around town playing kinky games with one another? Anybody would've thought the same as you."

They both stopped to take a sip of their drink, both exclaiming at the sweet tart taste that hit the spot as the alcohol coursed through their systems and did what it did best.

They were both of the school of thought that a drink a day kept the doctor away.

"I wonder what's gonna happen next."

"What do you mean Constance?"

"Well, you know what they say Lenore, these things always happen in threes."

THE END
Coming Soon: Murder In A Small Town

Made in United States
Orlando, FL
12 July 2022

19683057R00126